THE RIGHT TIME TO DIE

Rohan Sharma Thrillers
Book Three

C. V. Chauhan

SAPERE
BOOKS

THE RIGHT TIME TO DIE

Published by Sapere Books.

24 Trafalgar Road, Ilkley, LS29 8HH

saperebooks.com

ISBN: 978-0-85495-395-0

To the memory of my father and my mother:
Vallabhbhai Chauhan and Sitaben Chauhan

.

ACKNOWLEDGEMENTS

I am deeply indebted to a number of individuals who read early drafts of this novel. Linda Cook, Helen Dhillon and Susan Kent gave freely of their time and helped me to shape this book. I am also grateful to Yvonne Elizabeth Scott, a reader who contacted me and who drew my attention to the existence of a large sanctuary for tropical birds in Leicestershire. I visited Tropical Birdland in Desford and spent a pleasant afternoon there, enjoying the company of many tropical birds, including African grey parrots. As a result, some of the story relating to DI Sharma's pet parrot, Fernando, is located there, although I use a fictitious name for the sanctuary in the main body of the book. Thank you, Yvonne, and all the staff at Tropical Birdland! As ever, my profound gratitude goes to Amy Durant and Matilda Richards at Sapere Books for their considerable editorial skills, and the continuing tact and wisdom with which changes were suggested. My heartfelt thanks to you all, although I take full responsibility for the final product.

PROLOGUE

Eighteen-year-old Zac Cavendish arrived at the bus stop at 6.55pm. It was a Saturday in mid-September and he was going to meet a small group of school friends in Newark-on-Trent, their final party before they set off to different universities. The plan was the usual: pub crawl, nightclub, kebabs.

Zac stood by the wooden shelter. He wasn't waiting for a bus but for a lift with Josh, Archie and Harry. A cold breeze ruffled his blond hair. He pulled his dark hoodie tight around his midriff. The leaves on the trees behind the shelter were already turning from green to orange, with some falling to the ground. The days were drawing in and, in the distance, he saw the traffic speeding along the A46 dual carriageway which ran parallel to the road he was on. The one he would soon be travelling on. The headlights of some cars were already on, the evening gloom descending as rain-bearing, cumulus clouds gathered high overhead.

His phone pinged. A text message from Josh: *Soz. Delayed. ETA now 7.20ish.*

Zac checked his watch. Half an hour to wait. He paced up and down, hoping it wouldn't get too dark too quickly. He saw a magpie land on the field behind him. One for sorrow. He shuddered. Superstitious nonsense. He shoved his hands deep into the pockets of his hoodie and stomped his feet on the cracked pavement.

He stared into the field behind the shelter and thought he saw movement through the gaps between the trees. He squinted. In the distance he saw two silhouettes, a man and a woman. A faint, feminine giggle floated through the air. They walked past a weed-covered slag heap, and paused at the entrance to the disused coal mine, ducking their heads as they went inside.

Zac smiled to himself. He bet he knew what they were up to. Zac looked at his watch again. 7.07pm. Josh and the others would not be here for another ten minutes or so. He wasn't doing anything except getting cold standing here and he wanted to know what was happening in the mine. Maybe even film it as a laugh to show the lads. He could be back here before the others arrived in the car, couldn't he?

He clambered over the low drystone wall and jogged quietly toward the mine, jumping over the babbling brook. The entrance to the tunnel was boarded up with old planks of wood but a gap to the side remained, enough to let a person through. 'Danger! Keep Out!' notices lay faded on the ground with twisted barbed wire pulled from the entrance. Shattered glass from bottles and crushed beer cans lay on the ground.

Zac climbed through the gap and stood for a few moments, blinking so his eyes could adjust to the gloom. He crept quietly along the tunnel and saw a red light in the distance. He could hear a woman's voice further ahead. A man laughing. Zac moved towards the light. It became brighter. He stopped and crouched when he reached a corner.

In front of him was a large rectangular cavern, marking the end of the tunnel. An infrared bulb hung from the ceiling, the low hum of an electric generator coming from somewhere. Two middle-aged men sat on canvas chairs in front of a low table. The couple he had seen entering the mine sat opposite them. They all stared at the screen of a mobile phone placed on the table, listening to a voice which sounded to Zac like it may have been Arabic. One of the men switched off the call, and said, 'Our source says the Magician is about to get all the components we need. Then we can show the world what we're made of.'

A cold chill ran down Zac's spine. This was not what he had been expecting, and he had a sudden desire to leave. He turned and crept back the way he had come, trying not to cough on the coal dust.

Just then his mobile trilled.

'What the hell was that?' said one of the men in the cavern.

'Someone's here,' said another man.

Zac ran as fast as he could towards the broken planks of wood and the fading light outside. His phone carried on ringing but he didn't stop. He made it to the end of the tunnel and in the distance he saw the outline of the wooden bus shelter.

Heavy footsteps sounded behind him and a voice bellowed 'Stop!'

Zac ran towards the road. It was pouring with rain as he jumped over the brook but he could see a pair of headlights in the distance coming towards him. It could be his mates. He was almost there.

His calf muscles felt like lead. His heart thumped against his ribcage and blood pounded in his ears.

He waved and shouted. 'Help!'

A fierce blow struck the middle of his back and propelled him forward. His legs buckled and he fell to his knees. He tasted blood and tried to speak, but only gurgled as air escaped from his chest.

The car slowed down and stopped in front of the wooden shelter. Zac's phone trilled again.

After a few moments the car drove off into the evening dusk.

CHAPTER 1

Three weeks later

It was a late Sunday afternoon in October. I was in a good mood as Captain Anita Thomas and I sat on the settee in my terraced house in north Leicester and sipped some tea, watching a mindless gameshow on television. She leaned over and kissed me tenderly. I smiled back at her. It had been a year since our paths had crossed. As a detective inspector with the Major Crimes division of Leicestershire Constabulary, I was working on a complicated case involving money laundering and human trafficking. Anita had become involved through her work with the Ministry of Defence. She was a human resources officer in the British Army and had made the first move, when the case had wrapped up.

We met for a meal, and things progressed quickly from there. We met as often as our work commitments allowed. It felt good to be in a relationship again, the first since my marriage had broken down four years ago, and I enjoyed waking up next to a warm body in the morning, even if it wasn't every day.

'Come on,' I said, getting up from the settee, 'time to go.'

'Do we have to, Rohan? Can't we go upstairs again, just for a little while…? It's lovely and warm in your bed.' She smiled.

As much as I wanted to do as she suggested, I didn't want to miss the Diwali celebrations. 'There'll be plenty of time for that later.' I took her hands and gently pulled her up to standing.

Fernando, my African grey parrot and best friend since childhood, stared at us from the perch in his cage. Without warning, he squawked, 'Anita sucks! Anita sucks!' and blew a wolf whistle.

I raised my voice and said, 'Fernando, don't say that!' as I saw crimson blotches sailing up Anita's neck. Fernando had had my undivided attention for a long time and was clearly jealous of my relationship with Anita.

I knew it would be very noisy outside once the fireworks started, which might upset Fernando, so I put on repeat one of his favourite pieces of instrumental music to soothe him: 'Albatross' by Fleetwood Mac. His eyelids immediately started drooping and his head swayed as Anita and I put on our coats and stepped outside.

The streets around my house had been closed to traffic for several days, as the decorations were put up and the stage was erected. Thousands of lights of various shapes and sizes and colours had been hung along the Golden Mile, famous for its Indian shops and restaurants, and would be ceremoniously switched on later.

As I double-locked the front door, I saw a familiar face walking towards us.

'Hello, Mr Gupta,' I said to my elderly South Asian neighbour, who was trudging slowly along the pavement. He wore a frayed woollen hat, the bobble at the top hanging by a single thread. He leaned on his walking stick and his rheumy brown eyes stared at me.

'Not seen you for a long time, Sharma *Sahib*,' he said. 'Been busy catching gangsters and murderers?'

'Just hoping for a quiet life, Mr Gupta. Hoping to enjoy the Diwali celebrations over the next few days.'

'I'm sure we'll all be doing that. Nothing bad happens around here. Thankfully,' Mr Gupta added, wiping his nose with the dark cuff of an old winter coat.

I gestured to Anita. 'This is Anita Thomas. My —'

'Girlfriend?' he interrupted, smiling and shaking her hand. 'I'm pleased. It isn't good for a young man like you to be living on your own.'

'My partner. We met many months ago when I was investigating a case involving organised crime. Anita's in the British Army.'

Mr Gupta looked at her and asked, 'Are you a Goan Catholic, with a name like that?'

Anita shook her head. 'No,' she replied. 'My family originally came from Kerala in South India. I was born in this country. We're Anglicans, though I don't go to church these days.'

'It's good to have a faith, Anitaben. Like us Hindus. It comforts us in times of need. And look at all these people around us.' Mr Gupta turned and waved his stick. 'All celebrating the victory of good over evil. Of Lord Rama and his wife Sita's defeat of the evil spirit Ravana.'

'Ah, well, Mr Gupta, we're off to watch the Diwali lights being switched on,' I said. 'I hope you enjoy the celebrations, too.'

We said goodbye and the old man continued along to his own front door in his scuffed brown shoes.

Anita and I walked towards the main road. The pavements outside the front doors were decorated in bright squares with vibrant colours. The vivid paisley patterns and others with lotus flowers, were designed to welcome Lakshmi, the goddess of wealth. Different geometric patterns in all colours of the rainbow were edged with *divas*, the Indian cotton wicks dipped in clarified butter, protected by glass cylinders to stop them from being blown out.

The people walking past us reflected the diverse community in Leicester: South Asian faces mingled with local white and Black people, along with curious Eastern Europeans who had not seen anything like this before. Anita and I joined the crowd milling along the Golden Mile.

I had initially wanted my two kids, fourteen-year-old Yasmin and ten-year-old Karan, with me on this important day. They had enjoyed Anita's company when we'd been out for meals, going to the cinema and daytrips during the summer holidays, and she enjoyed being with them. But my ex-wife Faye and I had eventually decided it would not be feasible, not only because of the roadblocks making the journey impossible, but because forty thousand people were expected for the celebrations and we both worried about their safety.

People jostled and pushed past us as Anita and I side-stepped the street jugglers and weaved around the fire eaters. We bought vegetable samosas and potato bhajis from the food stalls and then secured an advantageous spot on a high bench, not far from the brightly-lit main stage with two enormous video screens on each side.

The stage vibrated to the loud music and rhythmic thumping of the dancers' bare feet, all dressed in traditional Indian costumes. The women's bare midriffs betrayed goose pimples, while their wide expressive eyes, lined with black *kohl* and long lashes, opened and closed to the beat of the music. The numerous anklet bells jingled to the harmonies of the tablas, sitar and harmonium, played by musicians flown in especially for the occasion from Kerala.

As I scanned the undulating sea of faces from our vantage point, I felt myself tense.

'What's the matter, Rohan?' Anita asked. 'You seem uneasy.'

'Oh, it's nothing really. I just don't like large crowds. Part of my police training. Anything could happen.'

'You're too suspicious. Nothing is going to happen — look, people are having fun.'

The festival was indeed an exuberant affair, but I could still sense friction in the air. The recent hostilities between belligerent groups of Hindus and Muslims, airing grievances stretching back to the partition of India in 1947, had led to violence on the streets.

People had been afraid to go outside at night and even though my colleagues had arrested many of the troublemakers, there had been some no-go areas for the police.

The various far-right groups had been calling for demonstrations against this supposed lawlessness, especially in areas with large concentrations of South Asian people. They said they wanted the streets safe again and demanded mass deportations. The situation eventually subsided, but the veneer of cohesion between the different groups was tissue-thin, and likely to tear apart at a moment's notice. Word on the street was that some extremist Muslim groups had threatened to disrupt this Hindu celebration, with chatter in some dark corners of the internet about the use of bullets and bombs.

Looking around, I could see there were plenty of police officers in uniform in attendance, but I also spotted a number in plain clothes, both white and Asian. The officers were obviously trying to pick up local intelligence but I suspected they wouldn't be able to find out much tonight. Even though I lived in the area, I hadn't been asked for my views on what had been happening between the different groups, or to contribute to police intelligence in any way. But that seemed to be par for the course and it no longer surprised me.

As seven-thirty approached, the traditional dancing on the main stage stopped. Strobe lights swivelled and a drum roll commenced. The master of ceremonies, a local radio celebrity, strode on to the stage. The crowd cheered loudly.

'Ladies and gentlemen. Boys and girls. Can I have your

attention, please?'

The Wheel of Light slowed to a halt — faces peering down from the pods of the massive, illuminated Ferris wheel — and the music from the nearby recreation ground died down.

'Welcome to this joyous occasion,' the MC shouted.

I scanned the crowds. My right thigh was twitching up and down. Anita glanced at me. A helicopter flew overhead. Officers in riot gear were on standby in adjoining streets ready to be deployed quickly if needed.

I looked back at the stage.

'Get off! We don't want to hear you!' somebody shouted.

The MC ignored the comment and continued thanking the crowd, the local businesses, the council and all the other organisations that had contributed to the event.

There was unease and impatience in the air.

'So, without further ado, let's welcome Sunil Kumar, the man you've all been waiting for!'

There was wild cheering. 'About bloody time!' another voice shouted.

Sunil Kumar, Bollywood icon, star of more than sixty action films, strode along the main stage from the wings. The crowd clapped and whistled as security guards lined up behind the temporary railings to the front and sides of the stage.

Kumar raised his arms and blew air kisses, his dazzling veneered smile a permanent fixture. Then he gestured for quiet.

Eventually, the crowd settled down.

'*Bhaiyo aur behno*, brothers and sisters. Mothers and fathers. Uncles and aunts. Friends! It's a great privilege to come back to Leicester. They say this is the largest gathering of Hindus outside India. Apart from Mumbai, where I live, this is the only other place where my heart is.'

The crowd shouted and clapped. He certainly knew which buttons to press.

'It's an honour to be invited to switch on the Diwali lights. I walk behind other Bollywood giants who've had the same privilege…'

He carried on for a few more minutes, his smile glued to the TV cameras that were beaming his image all over the world, until the time came to switch on the lights.

'Let's count down together from five,' said Kumar. 'Five!'

'Four! Three! Two! One!' we all shouted.

He flicked on the dummy switch attached to the lectern on the stage. Six thousand decorative lights strung from lamppost to lamppost, stretching all the way down the Golden Mile, came to life all at once. Gold and silver lights in the shape of diamonds, circles and stars, the sun and the moon, dangled like giant daisy chains.

The crowd cheered. Children gazed in awe. The fireworks above the Wheel of Light exploded into millions of stars. I scanned the crowd. There was nothing untoward. I squeezed Anita's hand. She smiled. Her deep brown eyes reflected a kaleidoscope of swirling colour.

I looked back towards the stage. The pungent smell of sulphur and saltpetre from the fireworks hung in the air. Sunil Kumar raised his arms, wanting further quiet.

I stared at the giant video screens. The camera focused on Priyanka, Sunil's wife waiting in the wings. Bollywood's golden couple.

'*Bhaiyo aur behno!*' Sunil Kumar shouted.

'See,' Anita said, 'I told you nothing was —'

That's when the shots rang out.

CHAPTER 2

The sound of the shots reverberated around the buildings. Then everything happened in slow motion.

Three red dots appeared on Sunil Kumar's cream shirt. Then a spray of bright red blood arced across the stage. Some of it landed on the pale neck of a security guard facing the crowd.

The crowd stared at the stage. A deathly hush fell along the Golden Mile.

Kumar staggered back. He dropped to his knees, then slumped sidewards.

Someone shouted, 'He's been shot! Sunil's been shot!' Then pandemonium broke out.

There was screaming. People jostled and pushed, anxious to get away in case there were more shots.

I ran towards the stage. The MC stood frozen at the side. The security guards jumped up on the stage.

I followed and rushed over to Sunil Kumar.

He was struggling to breathe, but there was life in his body. His chest heaved.

'Sunil, an ambulance will soon be here,' I said. 'They'll take you to hospital. Try not to struggle... Please ... please just stay with me.'

A first aider from the St John Ambulance service jumped up onto the stage and squatted next to me. She opened her canvas bag, which was full of bandages and dressings, and pressed a thick wad to Kumar's chest in an attempt to stem the bleeding.

I stroked his forehead.

Behind me, the crowd ran in all directions, trying to get away. People were shouting at each other, calling out for loved ones.

'Please, Sunil. Please don't die,' I implored, as the first aider helped him.

Kumar opened his eyes. He looked up and winked at me. Then he whispered, 'Great performance, wasn't it?'

I frowned.

'The cameras,' he said. 'The TV stations. They'll beam this around the world…'

I looked at the first aider.

'This is wonderful publicity for me. The bullet holes, see; harmless.' He poked a finger through one of the holes in his shirt. 'I asked the special effects guys from one of my films to do them for me. The blood? Well, that is real. But it's animal blood. Obviously not human.'

I dropped his head and clenched my fists. 'You bastard!' I said through gritted teeth.

Kumar jumped up onto his haunches. It was like a scene from one of his kung fu films. He grabbed the microphone.

'People! People! It was a joke. I'm all right. See? Just performing a stunt.'

The crowd stopped and looked back at the stage, not sure what was going on anymore. An uneasy murmur floated on the cool evening breeze. Someone laughed nervously. Then others joined in.

'You bastard!' I repeated in a low voice. 'People could've died. There could've been a stampede.'

'Oh, keep your hair on. See, they love me.'

I turned round and trod firmly on his foot. Furious, I walked off the stage and found Anita.

Kumar addressed the crowd again. 'It was good, wasn't it? You'll remember that for a long time. You'll tell your children. And they'll tell theirs. People of Leicester, I love you!'

There was loud applause. Cheering. Whistling. The stamping

of feet.

'Oh, look, he's fallen down again,' said a woman as I started to walk away, hand in hand with Anita.

'Okay, Sunilbhai,' shouted a man in the crowd. 'You've had your fun.'

There was the sound of running feet on the stage.

'He's collapsed!' shouted one of the security guards.

Priyanka screamed.

I turned around. The crowd surged. The first aider knelt over the actor's prone body again. She ripped open the blood-stained shirt — there were no obvious wounds — and started performing CPR.

A woman in a grey hoodie rushed past me, shouting, 'I'm a doctor!' She took over from the first aider, pumping Kumar's chest. 'Somebody call for an ambulance!'

I pulled out my mobile phone and rang for an air ambulance. A road vehicle wouldn't be able to get through the crowd.

The helicopter arrived within a few minutes and landed on the dual carriageway not far from the stage.

'Come on, Sunil. Wake up. I love you, I love you,' Priyanka beseeched, as Kumar was stretchered off.

The air ambulance lifted off, swung right and disappeared into the night sky.

CHAPTER 3

The walk from the stage back to my house took a while as Anita and I struggled to push through the distressed crowd.

'I hope he's all right,' said Anita, as we entered the front door. 'What do you think happened, Rohan? You were with him.'

'I don't really know. He looked fit and healthy, not that I'm a doctor.'

'Well, the noise from the fireworks doesn't seem to have upset Fernando. Hello, baby.' She went to stroke his head. 'Ouch! He bit me.'

'Well, no love and peace for him,' I replied. 'You shouldn't disturb him.'

'He always bites me. Or screeches when he sees me.'

'It's only because he doesn't really know you. He'll be fine once the two of you are friends.'

My mobile rang.

'Hello, Rohan,' said my boss, Superintendent Breedon. 'I gather there was an incident at the Diwali celebrations?'

I explained what I had seen.

'We've got a problem at Leicester Royal Infirmary, Rohan. Hundreds of people are already gathering outside the hospital, not to mention the press. I also understand that prominent members of your … of the Hindu community are demanding to know what's going on. Superintendent Grant has asked for uniforms to attend.'

'What's all this got to do with me, Sir?'

'I think it would be a good idea if you got yourself up to the hospital. Use your inside knowledge of the situation.'

I sighed inwardly. 'I don't have any more inside knowledge than you do, Sir. Anyway, why are we getting involved? It looked like Sunil had a heart attack. No crime seems to have been committed.'

'Good PR, Rohan. We need to make sure we're seen to be supportive of the star and his family. Plus, we need to make sure the crowd's under control. We don't want any other incidents, if you see what I mean. Superintendent Grant needs to be relieved soon. He's been on duty all day. But he'll support you by phone if you need it.'

So, Breedon wants to set up a fall guy, in case anything goes wrong, I thought. 'A stool pigeon,' I said out loud, without thinking.

'What did you say?'

'Sorry, Sir. Stool parrot. That's what I call my pet parrot. He likes to perch on my stool.' This wasn't a complete lie. I did have a stool.

There was a brief silence before Superintendent Breedon asked, 'Can you tell me a little more about the actor?'

I explained that Sunil Kumar was adored by millions all over the world. He was often compared to Jackie Chan because he performed most of his own stunts.

'Like today, you mean,' replied Superintendent Breedon. 'Well, I've never heard of him.'

'Doesn't surprise me, Sir.' I didn't think Bollywood films were the superintendent's cup of tea.

'Just get to the hospital, Rohan.'

The line went dead.

'Shit!' I said. 'I'm really sorry, Anita. I've been ordered to go to the hospital. I was looking forward to our evening together.'

She looked crestfallen. 'Ah well, that's how it is, Rohan. We have to follow orders.'

I hugged her, not wanting to let go.

'I need to go back to Aldershot early tomorrow morning,' she said, 'so try not to be back too late. I don't want to be left alone all night. Not with psycho over there in his cage,' she added, nodding at Fernando with a grin.

Once I had made it out of the roadblocks by showing my police ID, I found the route leading to Leicester Royal Infirmary gridlocked with traffic. I parked my white Mercedes Coupé about a mile away and walked briskly to the hospital. I fought my way towards the main reception, flashing my badge at everyone blocking my way.

When I eventually entered the reception area, it was under siege. Uniformed officers and Sunil Kumar's bodyguards were keeping unauthorised people at bay. The hospital staff were clearly stressed, not used to dealing with a celebrity patient.

I was directed to the Intensive Care Unit, where I had been informed Kumar was being treated. There were two private security guards at the door, who let me in. The smell of disinfectant and serious illness hit me as I entered, making me feel slightly queasy.

A nurse informed me the office of the Indian Prime Minister had been in touch, asking about Kumar's condition, as had the office of the British Prime Minister. Phone calls were also being received from prominent politicians, from both the UK and India.

I asked the nurse if I could see the doctor treating Kumar but I was told he was too busy with his team trying to diagnose Sunil's condition. I nodded and instead went to find Priyanka Kumar, the superstar's wife. She was sitting in the nearby waiting room, her eyes red and swollen, a crumpled tissue in her hand.

She greeted me pleasantly when I introduced myself. I asked

her whether she knew what was wrong with her husband and she said she did not. I said I was keeping an eye on things, and then I left her to her anguish.

The chief executive of the hospital arrived to see me, having rushed back from home on a Sunday evening. He had asked the telephone engineers to set up a separate phone line for updates on Sunil Kumar's condition so that the switchboard could be freed up. I advised him to issue a holding statement to the media explaining the star's condition and how he was being treated. He nodded, obviously not having dealt with an incident of this magnitude before. Neither had I, but it seemed the best thing to do. Keep the press at bay. Feed them information, a bit at a time. Hopefully, the doctors would diagnose the problem quickly, treat Kumar, and after a few days in hospital we could all settle down again to a normal life.

My mobile rang and I had to go to the outside corridor to take it. It was my mother. She wanted to know how Kumar was doing. She had probably promised her friends she would get inside information from her son, the police officer, who was bound to know what was going on. When I told her I knew nothing she accused me of holding out on her and hung up. Then my daughter Yasmin rang, again wanting to know what was going on, and I had to disappoint her as well.

I paced up and down the corridor before taking a seat. The staff were busy and had no time to speak to me. It was getting late now and I wanted to go home and have a cold glass of Sauvignon with Anita, eat the fish pakora and chicken tikka we had bought, and then get back into bed like I'd promised her. I smiled at the thought.

'Inspector Sharma?' asked a man in a white coat, strolling towards my chair outside the ICU doors and snapping me out of my reverie. 'My name is Dr Hughes. I'm the consultant looking after Mr Kumar. I gather you wanted to speak to me?'

'Yes, Dr Hughes, thank you. I appreciate no crime has been committed but given the importance of your patient and the fact that there are hundreds of people outside, not to mention the world's press, my superiors thought it best if the hospital staff were supported by our presence.'

'That's very kind of you, Inspector. But I wouldn't jump to conclusions if I were you. Not yet anyway.'

'What do you mean?'

'Well, Mr Kumar is a very sick man, and it's not clear why. We've conducted a number of tests: an ECG, brain scan, blood tests. It's clear he didn't suffer a cardiac arrest and he hasn't had a cerebral haemorrhage, but his vital signs are fluctuating wildly and he has severe internal bleeding and hypertension. We're trying our best to stabilise his symptoms but I'm afraid the prognosis isn't good.'

I stared at the exhausted doctor's face. It wasn't the news I was expecting.

'What do you think happened to him, Doctor?'

'It's difficult to say with certainty at this stage, Inspector. We're waiting for a range of toxicology results to come back. We've sent some of the samples by courier to specialist pathology labs in London and Liverpool and it might take a couple of days to get the results back. I haven't said anything to his wife yet, but my team and I think there is strong evidence — given the nature of the symptoms — that Mr Kumar was poisoned.'

Shit, I thought, the cogs in my brain whirring. 'Do you have any idea what the poison may have been?'

'No firm idea at this stage, but the symptoms and their duration could indicate a poisonous plant.'

'Is he in any state to speak to me?'

'No, and he won't be for a while, if ever. He's on life support to give his vital organs a chance to recover. But, as I indicated earlier, it doesn't look good at this stage. In all honesty, there's not a lot for you to do here. It's late and I'd go home if I were you. I'll keep you posted if you leave your contact details at the desk.'

I thanked the doctor and then rang Superintendent Breedon.

A groggy voice answered. 'This had better be good, Rohan. I was fast asleep.'

I didn't apologise. 'It seems that Sunil Kumar may have been poisoned, Sir. The doctors are waiting for toxicology results. The results will probably take a couple of days, but we could have a big problem on our hands if anything happens to him, given his fame and, shall we say, connections.'

I could hear rustling as Breedon sat up in bed. I heard the bedside lamp being switched on.

'Can he be moved at all, Rohan? To a specialist hospital in London? Or ideally, be flown out of the country? Back home to India?'

'Sir, he's on life support. It's touch and go if he'll survive. I don't think moving him is the answer. We can't get rid of the problem if that's what you're thinking.'

'Your words, Rohan, not mine.'

'There are also hundreds of well-wishers outside the hospital. Not to mention the media. We need to manage this situation properly.'

There was a pause. 'Well, you know I've always had a high regard for you, Rohan, and it will look good on your CV if you deal with this case. You can be the senior investigation officer if anything untoward happens.'

He had jumped into his life raft and cast me adrift. Again.

'Now go home till the morning,' he continued.

27

I arrived home just after one o'clock. The lights were off and I was too tired to warm up any food. Fernando was in his cage downstairs, fast asleep. I tiptoed up the stairs. Anita stirred as I climbed into bed beside her. She turned, and cuddled up to me.

'Hi, Rohan,' she whispered. 'I'm sorry I couldn't stay up.'

I held her close. 'It's not your fault. Go back to sleep.'

CHAPTER 4

I woke up a few hours later, daylight piercing the gaps in the frayed curtains. I searched for Anita's warm embrace but the bed was empty. I dragged my tired body downstairs, half expecting to see her making a cup of tea and munching some cereal, but all I found was a note on the table: *Sorry, Rohan, I have to leave early. Need to be in Aldershot by nine. Will ring later. Lots of love xxx*

I felt guilty. I should have rung her last night from the hospital at the very least.

'Good morning, Fernando,' I said, as I opened the door to his cage.

'*Olé!*' he replied, full of gusto.

I stroked his head, which he pushed into my palm, rubbing his head gently. 'Like that, don't you?' If he was a cat he would have purred.

I cut up some fresh pear and pineapple pieces, refreshed his water tray, made a cup of tea and sat down at the table.

'Fernando, why are you so mean to Anita? She's always good to you.'

His big grey eyes, moist and ringed by tiny, gossamer-white feathers, stared back at me. He blinked. Lifted a piece of pineapple with his claw and put it into his beak.

'Well? What about Anita?'

He turned around on his perch, lifted his long tail, and pooped on the newspaper at the bottom.

'Oh, Fernando!'

After breakfast and a quick shower, I returned to the hospital.

It was mid-morning and the crowd had thinned out because people had to go to work, but a sizeable number remained, many of them Asian women, still weeping, still standing with lighted candles and *divas* in glass jars. They were mumbling prayers to their various gods, including Jesus Christ. *May as well cast your net far and wide and hope for the best*, I thought. The media were being kept at bay by uniformed officers.

I took a long detour through one of the back doors and eventually made my way to the ICU, not wanting to draw attention to my presence. As I entered the unit, Dr Hughes rushed over to me.

'I'm glad you're here, Inspector Sharma. Mr Kumar is drifting in and out of consciousness. He can speak a few words. I'm not sure how long this will last, but if you're brief, you can speak to him. Please try not to distress him.'

I followed the doctor into the unit. Sunil Kumar's face was ashen. Tubes had been inserted into his nostrils and there was a cannula in his left hand. Electrodes were taped to his chest. The monitor above his head indicated a low pulse and very low blood pressure. His breathing was laboured, his chest heaving.

I bent over him and touched his shoulder. He opened his eyes, which were bloodshot and dry.

'Mr Kumar, my name is Rohan Sharma,' I said gently. 'I'm a detective inspector with the police. I was hoping you could answer a few questions for me. The doctor may have told you that he suspects you have been poisoned. If that's the case, do you have any idea how that may have happened?'

Kumar's eyes stared back at me, trying to focus. He was not the same man I had seen yesterday, who was full of life, laughing and joking with the crowd, pretending to be shot.

He mumbled something that I couldn't hear. I bent down and put my ear next to his dry lips. I asked him to repeat what he'd just said.

'Eye, says... Eye ... did this...'

'What? Eye says?' It clicked. 'ISIS?' I asked. 'The Islamic State?'

He nodded. I was confused. What could the militant Islamist organisation have to do with this?

He gasped for breath. The red horizontal arrows on the monitor above his head were falling and the machine started beeping. Staff rushed towards the bed and ushered me out.

A few minutes later, Dr Hughes came out of the room. He removed his pale blue face mask, rubbed his eyes, and shook his head. He went to see Priyanka Kumar in the waiting room and I heard her wail. As I walked out, I saw her thumping Dr Hughes's chest before slumping into his arms.

I waited a long time in the vicinity of the ICU, wondering whether I could speak to Mrs Kumar. After a while one of the nurses informed me that she would like to speak to me. Priyanka was in the waiting room, her two bodyguards with her.

I sat down beside her and after offering my condolences on the death of her husband I asked if she would mind answering a few questions.

Priyanka stared at me in a daze, probably hearing my words but not quite understanding what was being said. She held her crumpled tissue in her hands, twisting and turning it, pulling bits from one end.

'Mrs Kumar, can you tell me what you and your husband did over the last few days? I gather you came here directly from India?'

The muscle under her left eye twitched. She was physically and emotionally exhausted. Eventually she said, 'What day is it today?'

'Monday. Monday afternoon.'

She looked down at her designer shoes. They looked incongruous with the state of her hair, mascara smeared down her face. It reminded me of Jackie Kennedy leaving Dallas Hospital with her husband's dried bloodstains on the skirt of her pink suit.

After a while she said, 'We left Mumbai Airport last Tuesday on an Air India flight to Dubai. We stayed at our penthouse suite at the Burj-Al-Arab Hotel, on Tuesday and Wednesday night. My husband had some business meetings. We then travelled to your East Midlands Airport by private jet — my husband chartered it — on Thursday and we arrived in the middle of the afternoon. Oh, and we had a brief stop in Prague to refuel.'

'Did you meet anyone in Prague?'

'No. We rested in the VIP lounge, had some refreshments, and left soon after. We didn't see or speak to anyone apart from the airport staff. When we arrived here, we booked into our hotel. Of course, the media soon discovered where we were staying and started gathering outside the hotel gates. But this is normal for us. We went outside to say hello to fans in the evening and my husband signed a few autographs before our meal.'

'Did your husband meet with anyone between Thursday evening and Sunday?' I asked.

'Nobody apart from our security guards and the hotel staff. He was on the phone a lot, though. He wanted to speak to people about a new movie project and was pitching it to companies who he thought might put up the money.'

'And what about you? What did you do?'

'I went to the hotel's gym and pool. Had a massage, that sort of thing.'

'What about food, Mrs Kumar? Did your husband eat anything different from you?'

'No, we both ate at the hotel, and we picked the same things. As practising Hindus we are, of course, vegetarians, and there weren't many options to choose from.'

I tried not to feel guilty about my own diet. 'Did Mr Kumar feel unwell at any time? Either before or after you arrived in the UK?'

'He complained of having an upset stomach on Saturday afternoon. But he kept on saying "the show must go on" and tried not to let it bother him. He didn't eat anything on Sunday. I felt his forehead yesterday and it was clammy but I thought it was just nerves. Turning on the Diwali lights was a big event and we couldn't let people down.'

'What about the stunt he pulled before the switching on of the lights? Pretending to be shot?'

'Oh, you know my husband. Always laughing and joking. He thought it would be fun.'

The use of the present tense didn't escape me. 'Is there anything else you can think of that might be relevant? Did your husband say anything to you?'

'He said he loved me.' Priyanka Kumar sobbed into her tissue. 'Please, Inspector Sharma, what happened to him? The doctors aren't telling me anything.'

'I'm so sorry, Mrs Kumar. Hopefully we'll get some answers before too long.'

CHAPTER 5

I arrived at Leicester Police HQ in the afternoon and sequestered an incident room for the case. I set up my laptop at one end of the long conference table and started searching online for information about Sunil and Priyanka Kumar. There was an enormous amount about 'Bollywood's Golden Couple', from their films — starring together and separately — to their millionaire lifestyle, with luxury homes not only in India, but also in London, Toronto, Los Angeles, and Sydney in Australia. Celebrity news sites dished up gossip on longstanding friendships with other Bollywood stars, prominent Indian politicians, and millionaire business tycoons around the world.

I was so engrossed in my search that I didn't hear the door open behind me. A hand tapped my shoulder, startling me.

'Hello, Sir. How're you?'

I looked up. 'Angie! How wonderful to see you,' I said, beaming.

Constable Angie Deacon had been seconded to my team on my first case, but we hadn't worked together recently.

'Good to see you, too, Sir. It's been a while. Actually, I've recently been promoted to sergeant and Superintendent Breedon's asked me to work with you.'

'That's fantastic, Angie. And congratulations on your promotion.'

I invited Angie to sit down and briefed her on the situation. I asked her to confirm what Priyanka Kumar had told me about their journey from Mumbai to East Midlands Airport, via Dubai and a refuelling stop in Prague. And to also ask for

CCTV images from the airport and the hotel where they'd stayed, and when they went out to meet the fans at the gates.

I then asked her to inform Ben Carter, head of forensics, and Jamie Shriver, the head of the IT unit, that we would need their help. 'Oh, and please ask the pathologist's office when they can perform the autopsy. Given the high profile of the victim we need this to be treated as an absolute priority.'

Angie made some notes and nodded.

'Can you also contact the media companies, both British and international, and ask if they can share any footage they have of Sunil Kumar between his departure in India and his eventual arrival at East Midlands Airport.'

'I'll get onto it right away, Sir,' Angie said. She took off her immaculately pressed jacket and hung it on the back of her chair, ran her fingers through her curly dark hair, pulled forward the internal telephone from the middle of the table and started making various calls. I continued with my online search.

'This is interesting, Angie,' I said, when she was between calls. 'It seems Sunil Kumar hadn't released a film for two years or so. The last one was called *The Avenging Fists* — I'm translating from the Hindi title — and by all accounts it didn't do well at the box office. No information on what else he's been working on. Assuming it took several months to film *The Avenging Fists* that would mean he hadn't worked on a film for the best part of two and a half years. That's a long time for a Bollywood star. Normally, they're making several films at once, dancing from stage to stage — literally in some cases — on different sets in Mumbai.'

Angie nodded. 'That does seem strange. Maybe he was heading into retirement?'

I frowned. 'I don't think so. When I spoke to his wife, she

mentioned he was on the phone pitching a new movie project once they arrived in the UK, so there must be another reason. I'll look into it later.'

I went on browsing. Social media was flooded with thousands of comments about Sunil Kumar's tragic death, with fans around the world plunged into grief. Some of the reporters on the Indian television networks had been waiting outside Leicester Royal Infirmary and were now 'live' on air outside the hospital, speaking in both Hindi and English. The BBC and Sky News in the UK were also giving the story a lot of airtime. Nobody could understand how a supremely fit and active superstar in his thirties could be dead. I came across plenty of wild and wacky theories about Kumar's death, but nothing that implicated ISIS.

Why would an Islamic extremist group want to target him? They were not generally known for carrying out such acts on celebrities. It didn't make sense to me.

While Angie was on the phone, I tracked down the first aider who had attended to Kumar on stage. Her name was Julie and when I rang her, I asked her to recount what had happened. There was nothing remarkable about what she said and it was how I remembered it.

'What about the woman who rushed onto the stage, Julie? Did you know her? She said she was a doctor.'

'I'm afraid not, Inspector Sharma. But she seemed to know what she was doing. We both took it in turns to do CPR until the air ambulance arrived.'

'Did you happen to notice if she had anything unusual in her hands?'

'I remember looking at the sparkling diamond ring on the third finger of her right hand. Not the wedding finger. But she wasn't holding anything.'

'Thanks for your help, Julie,' I concluded. 'I might be in touch again once I've had a chance to look at the video footage. There were plenty of cameras covering the stage and the event.'

'No problem,' she replied.

A couple of hours later, I decided to call it a day and told Angie to go home too. There was nothing more we could do until the toxicology reports came through and the autopsy had been performed.

I left the office and hopped into my car, eventually turning along the Golden Mile. The stage and the crowds were long gone, but the road was still brightly lit with sparkling, winking lights. They would stay on until the New Year.

At home I rang Anita and apologised for not speaking to her sooner.

'It's been a whirlwind, Anita,' I said. 'I still can't quite believe Sunil Kumar is dead.'

'Do you know any more about what happened? I've been following the news but they aren't saying much.'

I hesitated, but I knew I could trust Anita completely. 'There's nothing official yet, so don't tell anyone this, but the doctor at the hospital suspects Sunil was poisoned. We're waiting on the toxicology reports, but we're pretty sure this is a murder case.'

'And you're in charge of it?' Anita asked.

'Yes, I'm the senior investigating officer, at least for now. There isn't much to go on yet. Before Sunil died, he whispered something to me. It sounded like he was implicating ISIS, but I must have misheard because that doesn't make sense.'

'I wish I could be there to help,' Anita said.

'I wish you were here, too. Do you think you can come over

this weekend?'

'I'd love that,' she replied.

I sighed in relief. I would really value her support and advice on the case.

After hanging up, I poured myself a glass of Pinot Grigio and rang my kids. Yasmin put me on speakerphone so they could chat to me together. They were both fine, bored with school as ever, and wanted to know about the case. I said very little to them — there was no way I would trust them to be as discreet as Anita — and they lost interest in talking to me after that, quickly saying goodbye.

I put my feet up on my stool and watched some mindless programme on television with dinner on my lap. Fernando was perched on my right shoulder, a peanut in his claw. I dipped a shish kebab into a tangy mint sauce.

'Fernando,' I said, between mouthfuls. 'Your attitude towards Anita stinks. What have you got to say for yourself?'

'I love you, Rohan,' he replied, nuzzling his head against my neck. He stretched out his claw and offered me his peanut. I declined. He put it into his razor-sharp beak and sliced it in half, crunching it loudly in my ear.

CHAPTER 6

The next morning found me in my boxer shorts and T-shirt, munching some muesli. Fernando was perched on the back of the chair next to mine and I flicked a raisin to him. He trapped it in his outstretched beak, both wings spread to aid his balance.

'Like that, don't you Fernando?' I said.

My mobile rang.

'Rohan,' said Superintendent Breedon. 'Hope I'm not disturbing your sleep? I'm already at the office.'

I heard the muffled bark of his dog in the background, which suggested he was lying.

'Of course not, Sir. I've been out jogging in Abbey Park for the last hour. Only just returned.' *Two can play at this game*, I thought.

'Well, that means you'll be fit enough to attend Kumar's autopsy at nine o'clock this morning. The Chief Constable's managed to persuade the pathologist's office to undertake this case urgently. She's had some prominent politicians pressurising her to find out what happened, given the importance of this actor. The Indian Prime Minister's office has also been in touch with Downing Street. We need to get to the bottom of this quickly, Rohan.'

The mortuary and autopsy suite were housed in an unremarkable brick building at Leicester Royal Infirmary. As I entered the building a few minutes before nine o'clock, the double doors to the autopsy room at the far end were flung open. The temperature dropped suddenly and a strong odour of disinfectant hit my nostrils. A South Asian woman dressed in a blue surgical gown, mask, cap and gloves, stopped and stared.

'Rohan? Inspector Rohan Sharma?' She pulled down her mask.

'Nasreen Khan?' I walked forward, shook her hand and smiled. 'What on earth are you doing here? I expected to see Dr Malik.' Malik was the forensic pathologist.

Like Angie Deacon, Dr Nasreen Khan and I had worked together on my first case. Sadly, she had had to leave Leicester before we apprehended the killer.

'Dr Malik left a while ago. Went to Leeds, I think,' she said, and smiled back at me. 'But I'm really pleased to see you. I wanted to get in touch since I came back, but I've been busy. You know what it's like — settling in, getting to know new colleagues and so on.' She looked at me. 'I'm glad to be working with you again.'

I smiled. 'So am I.'

'Poor Sunil Kumar. Not a great actor in my opinion, but what a handsome man. I tried my best to save him on the day —'

'What?'

'When he collapsed on the stage. I performed CPR until the air ambulance arrived.'

'Were you wearing a grey hoodie?'

'Yes. Were you there?'

'I was, you ran straight past me.'

'Sorry, Rohan. I didn't notice you.'

Well, that solved the mystery of who the doctor was. I could rule her off my list of suspects. I looked at Nasreen's left hand. The first aider had been right. Nasreen's wedding ring was missing. When I had worked with her previously, she had been married, but her husband was a thug and had been abusing her. With the help of colleagues in the force specialising in domestic violence, I was relieved to see it looked like she was finally free of him.

I followed Nasreen into the post-mortem examination room and entered the viewing booth. It had a glass partition and a microphone to speak to the pathologist if necessary. I looked at the steel mortuary table, on which lay Sunil Kumar's naked body. Sterilised instruments were already laid out on a surgical tray. A young assistant was taking photographs of the corpse from different angles. A video recording was also being made of the procedure, and Nasreen began detailing her observations.

She examined every inch of the body minutely using a large magnifying glass. She paused at the right arm, near the bicep muscle, and then said from behind her surgical mask, 'Now this is interesting. The skin's been pierced. The puncture wound is about two millimetres wide. Possibly a fine needle, like the kind used for a vaccination... The skin around the wound has started to heal and is also slightly discoloured. It could be several days' old. We'll have to conduct further tests.'

I looked away when the hum of the electric saw started and when Nasreen lifted the large bone cutters and rib shears. The heart, liver, kidneys, stomach and other internal organs were removed, weighed and recorded.

After several hours, Nasreen and her assistant were finished. The pathologist came to find me.

'I know you won't be able to say much until the results are through, Nasreen, but any preliminary thoughts?' I asked her.

'There was a lot of internal bleeding in the stomach and intestines. He must have been in agony before he died. No evidence of cardiac arrest. Vital organs seem to be okay.' She hesitated. 'It seems highly likely he was poisoned. Possibly injected with something in the right shoulder, but that seems an odd place for it if it was a legitimate injection. Medical injections would be done lower on the arm.'

'Would the poison take effect straight away?' I asked.

'Probably not. It could have taken a while to work its way into his bloodstream from the injection site. He was probably poisoned two or three days before he experienced any symptoms. Last Thursday or Friday would seem a good bet.'

'Kumar arrived in the country on Thursday. If he was poisoned on that day, then it could have occurred in Dubai, or on the plane, or even when he landed in the UK. Any idea about the poison used?'

'Could be one of a number. Sorry, Rohan. You'll have to chase the toxicology department. I need to get washed and scrubbed for the next case but I'll let you have my report as soon as it's ready.'

CHAPTER 7

It was early afternoon as I drove my white Mercedes back towards HQ. I passed by shops selling second-hand furniture, cheap carpets, and fruit and vegetables which had seen better days. Men sat on low walls, smoking, frayed like the furniture they were forced to buy. One or two stared at my passing car.

My mobile rang. I pulled into a layby and left the engine running as I answered.

'Hello, Mum. How are you and Dad?'

'We're fine, *Beta*. Have you eaten?'

'Yes, Mum, I have. You didn't ring to ask me that, did you?'

'Is it true that Sunil Kumar — such a handsome man and such a wonderful actor — is it true that he died from a poisoned raisin?'

'What? What're you talking about?'

'Raisin. A poisoned raisin. That's what they're all saying on the Indian news channels. And on the TV stations. Listen to *Sunrise Radio* or *Radio Leicester*.'

I tuned into one of the stations where there was a special announcement.

'*...preliminary toxicology results suggest Sunil Kumar was poisoned with ricin. It is not known how or where the poison was administered. Ricin is a natural toxic protein which comes from the castor bean plant. When purified it becomes a water soluble powder. If inhaled or injected, symptoms start within eight hours and include coughing, fever, nausea, and breathing difficulties. There's also severe internal bleeding. The patient develops respiratory failure and shock, and usually dies within thirty-six to seventy-two hours...*'

Ricin. Not raisin.

'Mum, I've got to go,' I said. 'I'll call you later.'

I remained in the layby as the announcer continued: '*Superintendent Breedon of Leicestershire Constabulary has issued a statement. "We are deeply sorry about the sudden death of Sunil Kumar, a great actor and idol to millions. Indeed, I have seen some of his films myself. Our thoughts continue to remain with his family and friends during this sad time. It is unfortunate that the initial findings of the toxicology test results have been released prematurely. And certainly not by us. However, be that as it may, we have a highly skilled team investigating the case led by Detective Inspector Rohan Sharma. I have every confidence that DI Sharma and his team will get to the bottom of why and how Mr Kumar passed away. Thank you."'*

I switched off the radio and rang Superintendent Breedon.

'What the hell's going on … Sir?'

'Ah, Rohan. Glad you've rung. Somebody from the labs in London or Liverpool leaked the preliminary toxicology report — the one requested by Dr Hughes at the hospital — to a journalist at one of the Indian news channels. The switchboard here has gone crazy with people wanting quick answers. I had to engage in damage limitation. I didn't want to disturb you while you were in the autopsy room.'

'Even I didn't know it was ricin,' I said.

'Well, now you do.'

I stormed into the incident room and slammed the door shut behind me.

'Are you all right, Sir?' asked Angie.

I hadn't seen her sitting at a desk by the window.

'Sorry, Angie. Didn't realise you were there.'

'Can't say I blame you,' she said, with half a smile. 'I'd feel the same.'

I sat down wearily at the end of the conference table, with

the large video screen behind me. 'Guess you've heard, too.'

She nodded.

'Let's leave the cause of death for the time being, Angie. Till I process what's going on. Given the timescales involved, maybe Kumar was poisoned outside the UK. Maybe in India or even Dubai or Prague. Or even seven miles high above the Mediterranean. Then it may not be our problem.'

'Or it may be,' said Angie, with a resigned look. 'I've been going through the last known movements of Kumar and his wife. The video images are from various Indian news channels and some of the more famous international ones like *Al Jazeera* and *CNN*. I asked for all existing footage to be streamed to us, not just what's on social media or catch-up TV.'

Everything seemed to be as Priyanka Kumar had said. The couple boarded an Air India flight at Mumbai Airport at two o'clock in the afternoon, Indian time, the previous Tuesday and had a brief refuelling stop in Prague. They landed at Dubai after three o'clock, accounting for the time difference. There wasn't much footage of them in Dubai — just the odd video clip on social media posted by people who had spotted them shopping or going into the luxurious Burj-Al-Arab Hotel. The couple looked happy, Kumar shaking hands with fans, signing a few autographs.

There was some footage on *Al Jazeera* showing them at Prague Airport, making their way to the VIP lounge before boarding their private jet to East Midlands Airport. These images were taken by fellow passengers who had posted video clips on social media.

Angie had confirmed with Dubai Airport that the private jet had left at ten o'clock on Thursday morning, and landed at East Midlands at about three thirty in the afternoon. There was further footage of the couple on the local BBC news programme outside their hotel in Leicester, greeting fans just as the daylight was fading.

'So to conclude,' said Angie, 'I've scrutinised all the available video footage and there is nothing to suggest anything untoward. Kumar doesn't eat or drink anything that looks suspicious, unless he was poisoned on one of the planes or at the Burj-Al-Arab Hotel?'

'He may not have been poisoned by something he ate. The autopsy found a puncture wound in his upper right arm, which indicates that the ricin might have been injected. We're waiting for confirmation on that.'

'That changes things,' said Angie. 'Although, it should make it easier to spot if someone had to get close enough to inject him in the arm. I'll keep looking.'

'What about the CCTV from the hotel here in Leicester?' I asked.

'Two DCs went to get the hard drive. I asked them to bring it here, in case there's any evidence on it. It's being copied by Jamie as we speak.'

'Good thinking, Angie.'

Her bright blue eyes sparkled.

'Let's look at the local news coverage, both BBC and ITV. They had cameras outside the hotel, didn't they?' I asked.

'Yes, they did. Along with the Indian channels. The footage is mostly the same.'

The Regency Hotel is situated in a quiet and leafy village to the north of Leicester. The converted Georgian mansion, set in acres of green fields, has a long drive leading to a pair of heavy, wrought-iron gates. The cameras show dozens of people outside these gates, mostly young South Asians in their twenties and thirties, screaming in delight as the famous couple walk towards them.

The gates open and Sunil and Priyanka Kumar walk through. The crowd surge forward and security staff join arms to keep them back. Many of the fans wave autograph pads to be signed. Sunil Kumar, dressed in a dark navy suit, turns to look at his wife and she gazes lovingly back at him. He pulls out a dark pen — it looks like a felt tip — from his breast pocket, grabs an autograph pad, signs it and moves on to the next one.

An old DVD of one of his hit films is waved at him and he signs the plastic cover of that, too. The crowd surges. The couple smile, mime a thank you, blow kisses and wave. The cordon of security guards struggle to keep the fans at bay. A man in a saffron turban, holding a notebook and silver pen, is jostled forward and bumps against the star as the bodyguards rush to protect him. He mouths an apology, asks for an autograph. Kumar winces momentarily and rubs his right arm.

'Pause it, Angie! Pause!' I shouted, and stood up. 'There! That's when it happened,' I said, pointing at the screen. 'Run it again, please. And this time, go through it frame by frame.'

There was no doubt. We could only see the man in the saffron turban from the side, so it was difficult to make out his facial features, but he had a well-groomed beard. He was dressed in a white *kurta* with a black waistcoat. A beige pashmina shawl covered his right arm and shoulders. He could have been in his thirties or forties. He held the notebook in his left hand and a silver propeller pen in his right. As he surged forward with the crowd, the tip of the pen was pressed firmly, and deliberately, against Kumar's right arm.

'Stop there, Angie. Zoom in, please… No doubt about it,' I said as I stared at the screen. 'The fabric of Sunil's jacket is being pushed back — exactly where the puncture wound was found in the autopsy.'

We continued watching. Kumar quickly scribbled his

autograph. He rubbed his arm and then smiled and carried on. The camera followed the couple and we lost sight of the man in the turban.

Just then, Jamie Shriver, the head of the IT unit, knocked and walked into the room.

'Thanks, Jamie,' I said, as he handed the hard drive copied with the Regency Hotel's CCTV images to Angie.

'There's not a lot to go on, Sir,' he said. 'Mostly empty corridors, cleaning staff working late, reception area with people coming and going.'

'Can you find footage of the main gates please, Angie?'

This time, the footage was from a higher vantage point, as the CCTV camera was mounted on a lamp post near the hotel's entrance. It showed the back of the couple, walking down the drive towards the gates as they slowly swung open, the crowd surging forward, the cordon of security guards. On the right was the man in the saffron turban. His face was clearly visible now.

'Angie, can you zoom in on his face? Enlarge it. That's perfect. Jamie, can you print this off and also create a version in Photoshop with the beard and turban removed — add some hair as you think fit. Bring us a few hard copies of both, please. As quickly as you can.'

Jamie left the room.

'Angie, please can you send a copy of this video to Ben Carter and ask if he and his forensics team can go to the Regency Hotel. Tell him to sweep the building and grounds for evidence. Better get yourself there too and inform the hotel manager of what we're doing. Seal the Kumars' suite and ask the CSIs to go through it with a fine toothcomb. Take some DCs with you and start interviewing any potential witnesses. Take the two photographs of the man in the turban Jamie is working on now and see if anybody recognises him.'

'Of course, Sir. I'll do that right away.'

'Please also circulate the two photographs of the suspect to all the major crime units around the country. We need to find this man.'

CHAPTER 8

It was late afternoon when Angie left, after handing me copies of the enlarged photographs. I stared out of the office window. The streetlights had flickered on, casting their pale glow onto the road below. Some people had finished work for the day and were leaving through the car park gates. I needed to think through all the available evidence and see what further lines of enquiry could be drawn up.

I sighed and wondered whether I had left enough food and water for Fernando. There was a knock on the door. I opened it.

'Hello, Inspector Sharma.' The woman flashed an identity badge. 'My name is Meena Patel and I am an attaché from the Indian Embassy, working out of our Birmingham offices. As you know, the Indian Prime Minister has been liaising with Downing Street and they, in turn, have been in touch with your Chief Constable. I've been asked to liaise with you.'

'Why? Oh, sorry. Where are my manners? Please, please sit down,' I pointed to a chair.

I was completely thrown. Neither the Superintendent nor the Chief Constable's office had informed me of this visit. But that didn't surprise me.

'Thank you,' she said, sitting down. 'Given Mr Kumar's fame and his political connections to the governing party in India — let's not beat around the bush — we thought it best if Priyanka is asked to move to a private flat in Birmingham. We'll look after her. She doesn't have any family in this country. She and her husband have friends in Surrey and they have agreed to come up and support her. They may take her back to their mansion. No reason for her to stay here in Leicester, is there?' She raised her waxed eyebrows, and the small crimson dot on her forehead danced.

'No, no,' I replied. 'Not once we've asked her a few more questions. Might be best if she stayed at a hotel tonight and then go with you tomorrow. That will give my sergeant a chance to speak to her.'

'Okay, thanks,' she said, about to stand up. 'I'll call you in the morning.'

'Before you go, Miss Patel —'

'Meena, please.'

'Before you go, Meena. Do you have any idea why anyone would want to kill Mr Kumar?'

She shook her head. 'No. Maybe it was a disgruntled fan? Like the killer of John Lennon? Or someone jealous of his success? Your guess is as good as mine.'

'What about this man?' I asked, showing her the photograph of the man in the saffron turban. 'Any idea who he is?'

Meena looked at it carefully, then handed it back to me. 'No, sorry.' She changed the subject. 'We need to make arrangements for the body to be flown back to India for the funeral. The Prime Minister has declared two days of national mourning for Mr Kumar, who he has dubbed "the great Hindu hero". Can you let me know when the body will be released?'

'I'll get back to you on that as soon as I can, Meena,' I said.

She nodded and left the room.

The Prime Minister had referred to Sunil Kumar not as a great 'Indian' hero but a 'Hindu' one. That was an interesting choice of words, and perhaps contained a veiled insult to Muslims? I was thinking about that when there was another knock on the door.

Dr Nasreen Khan walked in.

'Nasreen, how lovely to see you again. Twice in one day. It must be my lucky day. What brings you here? A desperate desire to be in my company?'

'I was about to say flattery will get you everywhere, Rohan. But you ruined it with that last comment.'

I smiled at her.

'I needed to discuss the autopsy results of another case with one of your colleagues and I thought I'd drop by and see you, too. It's not a social call; I've got some important news for you.'

I looked at my watch. 'It's getting late,' I said. 'Do you fancy having a drink at *Raffles*? We can find a quiet corner and discuss things there?'

'Oh, I don't know, Rohan, what would my mother say? After all, I'm a nice Muslim woman. I'm not meant to drink alcohol.' She grinned. 'But what the hell! Come on. It'll be nice to catch up properly.'

Raffles was the local pub where most of my colleagues headed. Its proximity to our headquarters and the nearby Fosse Park shopping centre served by the M1 motorway meant it was generally busy during weekdays. A steady stream of people also booked into its restaurant during the evenings, from places as far as Nottingham, Coventry, Derby and Northampton.

Nasreen and I both ordered a large glass of white wine from the bar and then chose a secluded corner table, next to a wide wooden beam, the area lit by the warm glow of a cream bulb dangling above our heads. The round table was covered in a patterned cloth and an empty wine bottle in the middle held a pink candle, the flame flickering, wax dripping slowly down the sides.

'What exactly is this?' I said, as she handed me a ten by eight photograph. The object in the photo looked like a silver mushroom whose stalk had been squashed at the bottom. Serrated edges were carved all the way round the head. It lay on its side and was photographed against a pale background. I turned it this way and that, trying to work out what I was looking at.

Nasreen said nothing.

'Looks like a pellet of some sort,' I eventually said. I looked up and saw the dancing candle flame reflected in her bright brown eyes.

'Yup,' she said. 'The pellet we retrieved from Sunil Kumar's right arm. Made from a metal alloy. Probably platinum and iridium — I'll explain why in a minute. We've sent it off for analysis. The image has been magnified twenty times. So in reality, it's less than two millimetres wide. We're waiting for our own toxicology results but I agree with the leaked report. The symptoms described — and what we found in Kumar's body — are consistent with ricin poisoning. It seems the ricin was pumped into this pellet. It was then released slowly into the bloodstream.'

I told Nasreen about the man in the saffron turban with the silver pen.

'Yes, he could've used that to fire the pellet into the victim's arm,' she said. 'The pen could have had a sophisticated mechanism inside to do just that. Ideal for delivering a poisoned pellet, just like the tip of an umbrella.'

I must have looked confused because she continued, 'You know — the case of Georgi Markov, the Bulgarian journalist?' She tucked a strand of her dark hair behind her ear.

I shook my head. 'No, should I?'

'I had to study the case as part of my training. Markov was a dissident writer based in London and working for the BBC. In

1978 he was waiting at a bus stop near Waterloo Bridge when he felt a sharp sting on the back of his right thigh. He turned and saw a man picking up an umbrella, who then rushed off across the road, got into a taxi and disappeared. A small red pimple developed on his thigh and later that evening he became feverish and was admitted to hospital. He died four days later. Markov told doctors he thought he'd been poisoned. It was only after an autopsy that the pellet was discovered. The symptoms were consistent with ricin poisoning.'

'So, the pellet was fired through the umbrella tip?' I asked.

'Yes,' she replied. 'A sophisticated operation. Probably masterminded by the KGB because the Bulgarian Secret Service didn't have access to that kind of technology. Very painful way to die.'

I sighed. 'Where the hell do we go from here?' I asked, wondering if Sunil Kumar had perhaps been killed by the agents of a state. From the video footage I had seen earlier, it looked more like the actions of a crazed fan.

Nasreen downed the last of her wine. 'I don't know about you, Rohan, but I need to get home. Got plenty of things to sort out in my new house.'

'Before you go, Nasreen, I wanted to talk to you about something else.' I took a breath. 'I'm seeing someone. She's called Anita. She's an army captain and her work keeps her busy, but we try to meet whenever we can. It's still early days for us.'

Nasreen looked at me. 'I'm really pleased for you, Rohan. You deserve some happiness... But what has that to do with me?'

'Well, I need some help. You know my parrot, Fernando? He seems to be jealous of my relationship with Anita. He keeps biting her and making nasty comments.'

'Rohan, for God's sake, he's a parrot. You need to show him who's boss.'

'I know you're right, Nasreen. But he's my friend. I don't want to upset him.'

She stood up and put on her coat.

'And what about you? Are you with somebody?' I asked.

'You have got to be kidding. I've had enough of men. I don't want anyone in my life right now. Not even a parrot.'

CHAPTER 9

A few days later, I was summoned to Superintendent Breedon's office. He gestured for me to take a seat.

His starched, dark blue uniform was immaculate. The epaulettes on his shoulders gleamed in the bright autumn sunlight piercing the window behind him. He moved a black wooden figurine a few inches to the left on his large teak desk. A framed photograph showed the same figurine being presented to him by one of the First Nation tribes in Australia. He had been proud to receive it on his recent visit to Melbourne, talking about modern policing in a multiethnic community. He made sure the mainstream media covered the story.

He leaned back in his chair and smoothed his salt and pepper moustache with his fingers. 'The Chief Constable has decided,' he said, 'given the high-profile of the victim and the possibility that a hostile group was involved in his death, that the counter-terrorism unit should be involved.'

'Does that mean I'm no longer the SIO?'

'No, no, Rohan. You're still the senior investigating officer. The Chief Constable just wants the CT unit involved as well. As you know, there's a lot of tension on the streets.'

He looked across the desk. 'There is a lot of chat online between Hindu and Muslim groups. The Hindus believe Mr Kumar was murdered by the Muslims. Thank goodness there's been no leak of Mr Kumar's final words to you.'

I had briefed him previously on Kumar implicating ISIS. 'There's no evidence he was poisoned by Muslims, Sir, so I'm not sure how much attention we should pay to that. Anyway, the suspect appears to be a Sikh man, assuming the turban was genuine.'

'Be that as it may, an officer from the CT unit will work with you.' He levelled his cold blue eyes at me.

'What about the National Crime Agency?' I asked. 'Don't they want to be involved as well? The more the merrier as far as I'm concerned.'

'Don't be facetious, Rohan. We're trying to keep them at bay. They'll want the limelight.'

I raised an eyebrow, but he didn't respond.

As I closed the door behind me, I was frustrated to be left as the whipping boy should things go wrong, and now someone from the CT would interfere with my investigation when it suited them.

I walked down the stairs to the incident room, where Angie was waiting. After the usual pleasantries, I took a seat at the conference table and asked her to switch on the large video screen and computer. Today was an important day.

Since Kumar's cause of death was clear — all the test results confirmed ricin poisoning — the coroner had released the body. It had been flown back to India in a private jet, where thousands of people had been waiting at Mumbai Airport for the return of their martyred star. They had accompanied the slow-moving hearse to the mortuary and then a day later to the home of the actor, where the final funeral rites were performed. Now, the shrouded body had been laid on a large sandalwood pyre on the banks of the River Ganges in Varanasi, the spiritual home of more than a billion Hindus, and Angie and I were tuning in via the internet on a laptop to watch the final farewell.

An aerial view of the river showed tens of thousands of people, mostly dressed in white, the colour of mourning, wailing and beating their chests. The Indian Prime Minister and other senior politicians, dressed in the traditional white cotton kurta pyjamas, held their palms together in supplication, mouthing prayers. A little further back stood the expensively clad glitterati from the Bollywood scene, many in dark glasses.

The crowds were pushed back by khaki-clad police officers with sticks and security forces with guns as Priyanka Kumar approached her late husband. She held a brightly lit burning branch and, with her right arm shaking, lit the funeral pyre. The sandalwood logs, drenched in vegetable oil and clarified butter, quickly caught fire and the bright yellow flames danced towards the heavens. A solemn hush descended among the mourners. The thick smoke rose and the wood crackled.

Priyanka wept uncontrollably as she was led away.

High above the flames, the vultures cruised on the warm thermals, waiting to swoop down later on the cooling bones and burnt flesh.

My mobile rang and I asked Angie to stop the broadcast.

'Good morning, Mum. I'm at work. Is it urgent?' I braced myself.

'We're watching the funeral on the television. It's so sad. Mr Kumar was such a wonderful man. Your father and I have been praying for his soul. Why would the beef-eating heathens want to kill him?'

'Mum, please don't say that. You are being ignorant. We don't know who killed him.'

'Well, there are plenty of people in the temples and community halls here who believe the *mullahs* did it.'

'Sorry, Mum, I've got to go.' I ended the call with a sigh. 'Could be more trouble on the streets tonight, Angie; it seems the blame game is building. Let's catch up on what we've got so far.'

Just then, there was a knock on the door. I turned round as it opened.

'Tim! Come in, come in.' I rushed over to shake the hand of the tall man who entered. 'How're you? It's been so long.'

'Good, Rohan. How about you?'

'Angie,' I said, turning round. 'This is Detective Inspector Tim Lafferty. We were sergeants together in the dim and distant past. We did our DI training together. Tim joined the counter-terrorism division when I went into major crimes. Tim, this is Sergeant Angie Deacon.'

Angie stood up and they shook hands.

'I'm hoping you've been sent to work with us, Tim?' I asked.

He nodded in confirmation.

'What about Lisa? How is she?' I asked.

'A bit big at the moment. Seven months pregnant. Sorry about you and Faye. I heard you two had split up.'

I shrugged. 'I'm so pleased for both of you,' I said. 'Please say hello to Lisa for me. We must get together sometime.'

He agreed and we settled down to business. After going through the details of the case so far, I asked Angie to update us on recent developments.

'Ben and his forensics team did a thorough sweep of the Regency Hotel grounds and the suite Mr and Mrs Kumar were staying in,' she said. 'They didn't find anything of interest. Just the usual — fingerprints, all accounted for, and no suspicious DNA to speak of. The DCs and I interviewed all the relevant staff. Their version of events — who was on the premises and when — tallies with what we already know. House-to-house enquires — not that there are many in the area — yielded nothing of interest. I set up roadblocks, asking passing motorists if they remembered seeing anyone or anything suspicious, but once again, there was nothing forthcoming. I've shown Jamie's photographs to various people, but no one remembers seeing *The Turbanator*, either before or after the poisoning.'

I grinned. 'Great name for our suspect, Angie.'

'It seems,' she continued, 'that he came along, did the job and then disappeared. Nobody seems to know anything about him.'

'I think I might be able to help,' said Tim. 'Once we got whiff that a terrorist group may have been involved, we started gathering information. One of our "grasses" — or covert human intelligence source, to give them their proper title — contacted our intelligence unit this morning. He claimed to recognise *The Turbanator* —' Tim winked at Angie — 'and said he is an Islamic extremist. He was once a member of Al-Qaeda, then went over to ISIS, and has raised a lot of money for other extremists based in London. Apparently, he's a loner and has many aliases.'

I nodded. It seemed that Sunil Kumar's last words to me may have been right after all. 'Do we have a name for him?'

'Not one we are certain is real,' Tim replied, 'so we can carry on dubbing him *The Turbanator* for now.' He smiled before continuing. 'Because I knew we were going to work together, I sent a patrol car round to his last known address, but there's no one there. The house has been empty for a long time. None of the neighbours have seen him recently or know where he is now.'

Just then Tim's mobile rang. He looked up sharply. 'A body has been found and it sounds like our suspect.'

'Right. Come on then, team, let's go.'

By the time my Mercedes skidded to a halt on the tarmac outside the disused warehouse, three white forensic vans and two patrol cars were already waiting. Angie and I jumped out of the car as Tim pulled up in his.

The site was to the west of the city, a few miles north of police HQ on the road to Coalville and not far from the M1 motorway. Empty warehouses, mobile offices and a few brick buildings dotted the scene. Graffiti adorned most of the walls and the windows had been smashed a long time ago. The site was scheduled to be razed to the ground soon with a new housing development ready to take its place.

A large roll-over metal door to one of the smaller warehouses was open. Ben Carter and his team of forensic officers were already at work. They were dressed in white full-body suits and masks, some on their hands and knees, brushing the dust on the ground into plastic evidence bags, others walking around gingerly, dusting for fingerprints.

A cool autumn breeze ruffled my hair as we walked towards the warehouse. I pulled up the collar of my jacket, regretting not having worn a winter coat.

We entered the warehouse, voices echoing inside. There was a strong earthy smell in the building. I spotted Dr Khan, the pathologist. She was standing next to an upturned step ladder.

'Hello, Nasreen,' I said, walking over to her. 'Where's the body?'

She pointed up to the wooden beams supporting the roof. The body of a South Asian man hung from the crossbeam. He was wearing the same clothes we'd seen on the hotel CCTV images. One end of his saffron turban was wound tightly round his neck and the other end round the crossbeam. Blood had dripped from a wound to his back and there was also some on the front of his chest. The tips of his polished black shoes pointed down, splatters of dried blood on them. His hands, which once held an autograph pad and a silver propeller pen, were bound with plastic ties behind his back. I squinted up. Part of his beard had come away, revealing black and grey stubble. It had been a false beard.

A sudden gust of wind blew across the rafters and the old wooden beam creaked with the weight of the body.

I looked around. Some graffiti had been sprayed in black paint on the wall. It looked relatively fresh because it shone out against the peeling paint. A circle with the letter H inside. A lightning bolt went from the bottom left of the circle to the top right, across the H.

Ben Carter approached. 'Seems he was made to stand on the step ladder with the turban already round his neck. Then it's been knocked over. I will get you the report as soon as possible, Sir,' he said to me.

'We'll cut him down once Ben and his team finish,' Nasreen said. 'I'll get to work on him back at the Infirmary. It's not clear what caused the wound to his torso. The dried blood points to the fact that death occurred some time ago. Anyway, we'll know more in the next day or two.'

I thanked them both and asked Angie who had found the body.

'A local dogwalker called Martin Turner,' she replied. 'I'll take you to him.' She accompanied me to a disused mobile office. A middle-aged man leaned against the outside window, a King Charles spaniel next to him on a lead. Angie introduced me and I asked him how he found the body.

'I usually walk Jimmy in the fields over there,' he said, patting the spaniel and gesturing beyond the warehouse. 'But he kept pulling on his lead in this direction. So, I followed Jimmy down here and he started barking near the warehouse door and wouldn't come away. In the end, I looked through the window at the side and that's when I saw him... Scared the life out of me it did.'

I thanked the man and said we'd be in touch if we needed any further information. I asked Angie to make sure we had a full statement from him. 'Oh, and by the way, ask Ben and his team to sweep this mobile office for any forensic evidence. And get a message out on all the usual platforms. Say a body has been found and we're treating the death as suspicious. Any witnesses in the area, etc. I'm not holding out much hope of anyone coming forward though. Oh, and one last thing — make sure a photo of that graffiti in the warehouse is photographed.'

'Yes, Sir,' Angie replied. 'Will do.'

It was getting late, the daylight disappearing fast, so I decided to call it a day.

'Welcome home, Rohan, welcome,' said Fernando, jumping up and down on his perch when I arrived.

'Thank you, Fernando,' I said. 'You're very chipper today.' I took some mixed seeds, a piece of dried mango and a cashew nut and placed them in his food bowl.

'How're you, Rohan? How're you?'

'I'm dead beat. Or beaten by the dead. Take your pick.' I looked at Fernando, the beginnings of an idea taking shape. 'Fernando, from now on, if you want more fruit and nuts, you have to raise your wing. Like this,' I said, and demonstrated for him by lifting my arm up in the air.

Fernando stared at me, did a somersault on his perch, landed with his back to me, lifted his grey tail, and pooped on the newspaper lining his cage.

'Oh, Fernando! Is that your answer?'

He carried on eating the mango then dipped his beak in the water tray.

I went upstairs to change, came back down and caught up with my children before ringing Anita.

'Hello darling, how're you?' she asked.

'Missing you,' I said. 'Are we still getting together this weekend? I'm up to my neck in this case, so it'll be difficult for me to come down to see you for a while.'

'Well, I'm due to visit some barracks in the north next week. Maybe I can stay with you while I'm working there? Make up for lost time.'

'I can't wait.'

'And what about the resident psycho? Is he behaving himself?'

I laughed. 'Well, he doesn't misbehave when you're not here. Not much anyway,' I said, looking at Fernando, his grey, unblinking eyes boring into mine. 'I think he knows we're talking about him. Anyway, I'm trying to train him to be more obedient. You know, just like Pavlov's dog. If he wants food, he's got to associate it with something. With Pavlov's dog, it was the ringing of a bell. With Fernando, I'm going to try to get him to raise one of his wings.'

'All I can say, Rohan, is good luck. I'll catch up with you soon,' and she was gone.

Fernando flew across the room and landed on my shoulder. 'I love you, Rohan. I love you,' he said and nuzzled my neck, his body warm below the soft, grey and white feathers.

'You're still not getting any more food,' I said. 'You refuse to do what you need to do.'

After a while, he flew back to his perch, flipped around, lifted his tail and —

'Aw, Fernando, not again!'

CHAPTER 10

Mid-morning two days later, I was summoned to Superintendent Breedon's office. I walked towards the tips of the polished black shoes under the large desk. Without raising his head he finished scribbling something on a piece of paper, then pointed to the chair in front of him.

'Thought it'd be a good idea to have a catch-up, Rohan.'

I crossed my legs and then my arms. A defensive posture.

'I know you're making progress in the case. But we need it solved as quickly as possible. The Indian government is putting pressure on Downing Street, who are putting pressure on the Home Office, who are putting pressure on the Chief Constable —'

'— and she's putting pressure on you,' I concluded for him.

'There's trouble on the streets, Rohan. Tensions are running high. Some Hindu groups are blaming the Muslims for Kumar's murder. Muslim youths have been attacked and one young man is currently on life support at the hospital. Do we know who the main suspect is yet? If he's a Muslim or not?'

'No, Sir. Not at the moment,' I said, uncrossing my arms. I told him that an appeal had been put out, but that we had no leads so far. 'He was wearing a turban and a false beard, but that obviously doesn't mean anything at this stage. We might know a bit more once the team's had its briefing session this afternoon.'

Superintendent Breedon stared at me with his icy blue eyes. His moustache twitched. 'We're issuing statements calling for calm,' he said. 'And regular holding statements on the case, saying we're following up all leads and progress is being made in identifying the perpetrator or perpetrators. I have authorised extra patrols, including the neighbourhood where you live, Rohan. I'm trying to keep your name out of the media. Being a Hindu, we don't want anyone thinking you're taking sides. The NCA still wants to muscle in but we're managing to keep them at bay. For the time being.'

I met his gaze. I doubted the last statement. 'My team and I will go wherever the evidence takes us, Sir.'

He cleared his throat. 'If the suspect is a Muslim, we could have a full-scale riot on our hands. It could spread to other parts of the country. We need to wrap this up quickly. It could become dangerous for all concerned.'

For once I didn't disagree with him, although I suspected his motives were more self-preservation than anything else. 'Sir, if I continue leading on this case, I expect to be fully supported.'

'Yes, yes, Rohan. I'll support you.'

'Thank you, Sir,' I said, as I left the room.

After lunch, I strode into the incident room. Nasreen, Ben, Angie and Tim sat around the conference table, which was dotted with lever arch files full of papers. I sat down at the head of the long table with the large digital smartboard on the wall behind me. After welcoming everyone, I asked Nasreen to lead with her findings.

'The rate of decomposition of the body and evidence from livor mortis — the pooling of blood after death in the lower part of the body — would suggest the victim died several days ago,' she said. 'At least four or five, maybe more. Not long after Sunil Kumar died. The victim was shot in the back. The bullet pierced his body and exited from the chest. But that didn't kill him. It missed all vital organs.'

'My team found fragments of the bullet,' interrupted Ben

Carter. 'It came from a Smith and Wesson pistol, point three eight calibre. No sign of the handgun at the scene.'

'Our victim may have been shot and injured while trying to escape,' continued Nasreen. 'That would explain why he was shot in the back. The length of the turban used to hang him was too long to snap the neck instantly. He would have been gasping for breath for a long time before asphyxiating. There are severe bruises on both knees caused by a blunt instrument. It looks like he was hit there to make him jump off the step ladder.'

There was silence as we all absorbed the graphic description. A steady drone of traffic noise and the sound of air brakes from lorries could be heard outside.

'Jamie,' said Nasreen, breaking the silence, 'can you bring up your Photoshopped image of the victim on the board, please? The one without the turban and beard.'

Nasreen superimposed a photograph her team had taken of the victim's face onto Jamie's photographs. 'The images are almost identical. Interestingly, we found evidence that our victim had undergone a lot of plastic surgery, probably quite recently. His original nose has been made flatter, the ears have been pinned back, bags under the eyes have been added and the jowls have been puffed up too. There is still some fairly recent scar tissue. He — and the surgeon involved — went to a lot of trouble to change his facial features, I'm guessing to disguise himself. Anyone who knew him would probably still recognise him, but his passport photograph from before the surgery would not look like him now.'

'And we still don't know his identity,' I added.

'We have no evidence of him entering the Regency Hotel,' said Angie. 'And there are no CCTV images from near the warehouse.'

'Have you found anything else at the warehouse?' I asked Ben.

'We found a used condom in the mobile office,' Ben replied. 'It looked like it had been discarded fairly recently so we are running tests on it, but we haven't got a full DNA profile yet. Other than that, we haven't found anything of note.'

'What about the symbol sprayed on the wall?' I asked. Angie brought the image of the circle with the *H* and the lightning bolt up on screen. 'Any thoughts?'

'The black spray paint was fairly fresh,' said Ben. 'We're still waiting for a full analysis but I suspect it was only done a few days ago — perhaps sprayed at the same time as the victim was killed.'

There was a knock on the door and Superintendent Breedon walked in, accompanied by a woman in a smart suit.

'Hello everyone. This is Cynthia Thomas, from MI5. She's going to act as a consultant on this case. She has a lot of experience working with counter-terrorism units across the country.'

My surprise must have shown on my face.

'Sorry, Rohan,' Superintendent Breedon said. 'I didn't know about this when we spoke this morning. The powers that be made the decision. I'm sure Cynthia will be a big asset to the team.' He smiled and walked out.

'Cynthia!' said Tim Lafferty, walking towards her. 'Good to see you again.' He turned round and said, 'Cynthia and I have worked together before. We dismantled a few regional terrorist plots without news getting out.'

We all welcomed her. She went round and shook our hands warmly, the colourful beads in her dreadlocks shaking. She took a seat at the table and asked us to carry on.

Tim said, 'The lightning bolt is a symbol used by many

extremist groups, both the right and the left. Normally, it's two parallel bolts, not one, like the ones the SS used in Nazi Germany.'

'We monitor a lot of extremist groups on chat forums,' said Cynthia. 'We've seen that symbol used recently in Pakistan, Bangladesh, Bali, and the Philippines. Areas where there is increasing *jihadi* activity.'

'The *H* looks as if it could be an *A* to me,' said Angie. 'See the line at the top? Or perhaps it's supposed to show an *A* over the top of an *H*? Adolf Hitler's initials? Or is that too much of a reach?'

'Neo-Nazi groups tend to use symbols like *WP* for White Power, *4/20* for Hitler's birthday and *88* for *Heil Hitler*,' said Cynthia. 'I don't recall seeing that lightning bolt symbol appear within those groups. But you're right, Angie,' she continued. 'It could be an *A* and an *H*. We — that is my colleagues at MI5 — think it could refer to a man called Abdul Hussain. We don't know much about Hussain, if he's a Sunni or Shia Muslim, or where he's based, but we do know he's a wealthy individual and funds extremist activities around the world, and his name keeps popping up in chat rooms along with this symbol.

'And we know that guy,' she said, pointing a long pink fingernail over my shoulder to the photograph of *The Turbanator*, which was still on the screen. 'We have evidence of him participating in *jihadi* training camps in the deserts of the Sahel region in Western Africa, in Mali, and on the eastern coast in Mozambique. We think he may be Pakistani in origin, and he had access to large amounts of money through offshore accounts, usually in dollars, but also in other major currencies, including sterling.'

'If you and your colleagues were monitoring him, how come

he entered Britain without you knowing?' asked Jamie.

'Presumably, he paid for a new identity and a new passport. He could have entered the country by crossing the Channel. Not in a flimsy dinghy like the ones you see used by asylum seekers, but probably a yacht or a small ship, given the kind of people he associated with, which could have dropped him off at an obscure location in the middle of the night. Our borders are as porous as they come.'

Cynthia went on to explain that *The Turbanator* was in regular contact with a known drug baron in Pakistan named Mohammed Jahangir who supplied drugs to the UK. 'While monitoring Jahangir, we got information on another person of interest, who we now believe may be the second victim. They referred to him as Ali, but we don't believe that is his real name. We found out that Ali was in charge of arranging shipments of drugs for Mohammed Jahangir. We were tracking one of those shipment a couple of weeks before Sunil Kumar was killed, but the signal in the tracking device placed by one of our undercover agents died in Isfahan in Iran. We believe the shipment was due to make its way over to the UK. We don't yet have any intelligence on why Ali came to the UK or when he arrived.'

'Was the tracker discovered, or was it a technical glitch?' Jamie asked.

'We don't know for sure. The Iranians are good at sweeping vehicles for such devices. Chances are they found it and destroyed it.'

'So,' said Tim, 'what's the link between a known *jihadi*, an international drug smuggler, an Arab extremist and a Bollywood superstar?'

'We have no evidence yet that Sunil Kumar was involved in the drugs trade,' Cynthia replied, 'so we don't yet know why he was targeted. We're in touch with the Indian police and their internal secret service agencies, but nobody seems to want to say anything negative about the people's prince.'

The roads around my house were eerily quiet that evening. There were some pedestrians, one or two looking in the shop windows that were not boarded up, uniformed police officers walking in pairs. I knew my colleagues in riot gear would be waiting in parked vans in case they were needed. The air was tense.

I walked into the house and Fernando stared at me from his perch. He scratched the side of his head with a claw and a tiny white feather floated down.

'Hello, buddy. How're you?' I asked, gently stroking his head.

He flapped his wings and looked down at his empty food tray.

'I know, I know, I'll fill it up in a minute. Seeds and one piece of fruit and one nut,' I said. 'You know what you have to do if you want any more.'

He ate while I changed upstairs. I then poured myself a glass of Pinot Grigio, turned on the television, and decided I would make a chicken biryani.

While I prepared the ingredients, the film *Shawshank Redemption* played on one of the satellite channels. It had reached the part where the main character locks himself in the warden's office and plays an aria across the speakers to the entire prison, the voice of the soprano soaring over the exercise yard where the prisoners all look up, listening, because most had not heard anything like it before.

'That's an aria from *The Marriage of Figaro*,' I said, between sips of the chilled wine.

Fernando stared at the screen, dipped his beak in the water

tray, lifted his head high and let the water drain down his throat.

'But I suppose you prefer the *Parrots* of Penzance.' I laughed.

He squawked at my feeble attempt at humour.

'I know, it was a bad joke, but I don't have my kids to talk to.' I tried not to think about that. It felt like too long since I'd last seen them. As soon as this case was over, I'd spend as much time with them as possible.

I heated the rice, added cardamom and cinnamon, and was stir-frying some pieces of chicken when Fernando flew to the top of the television set and walked along the slim edge. 'Fruit and nut. Fruit and nut. Fruit and nut,' he squawked.

'You know what you've got to do. Raise one of your wings and you can have some. And don't you dare poop on the screen!'

He turned round and lifted his tail.

I sighed.

He flew back to his perch.

I cleaned up after him, ate my biryani from my lap tray and watched the rest of the film. I stood up to carry my tray into the kitchen and Fernando squawked. I stared deep into his round, grey eyes.

He grudgingly lifted his left wing, but not fully.

'Good boy, Fernando. But that's only half a lift. You can have half a nut for that.'

I walked to the dishwasher and started loading it.

Fernando squawked again.

I looked up.

His left wing was in the air, high above his body.

I smiled. 'Well done, Fernando. See, you can do it when you want to.'

I opened the cupboard and pulled out the bags containing

assorted nuts and dried fruit.

He blew a wolf whistle. 'I love you, Rohan,' he screeched, both wings flapping in excitement.

'I love you, too, Fernando. Oh, guess what? Your best friend will be coming to stay soon.'

He munched a dried apricot and gave me the evil eye.

CHAPTER 11

The next morning I was reviewing the evidence on the case so far with Tim when there was a knock on the door. Angie walked in. She looked at Tim, twirled a strand of her dark hair, then turned to me. 'Sorry to disturb you, Sir. Ben Carter's just contacted me. We've got a hit on the semen sample. Name of Gary Ashbourne. His DNA was already registered on the National Crime Database for previous theft and drugs charges. He's local, recently released from prison. I have his address.'

'Thanks so much, Angie. Let's go see him now. Tim, it'll be fairly routine, but you can tag along if you want.'

'No thanks. Got plenty to catch up on here.'

My car was conspicuous as I parked on a side street on a sprawling council estate in the north-west of the city. The warehouse where we found *The Turbanator* was about three miles away. We avoided the broken glass as we walked towards the line of pebble-dashed two-storey houses, separated by overgrown gardens and overflowing waste bins. Two youths in grey and blue tracksuits stared at us as we walked towards them, and as we skirted them, one of them spat loudly on the ground.

I pushed back the broken wooden gate that led to Gary Ashbourne's address and we walked up to the door. I knocked.

'Fuck off! Haven't got any!' came the shouted response from behind the door.

'Gary! It's the police. Open up!' I shouted.

Sudden silence. Then a scurrying behind the door. We waited.

'Come on, Gary. Open up!'

Eventually, the door cracked open a few inches. It was dark inside and a voice said, 'What the hell do you want? I done my time. I'm clean.'

'Gary Ashbourne?' I asked, trying to make eye contact. 'We need to talk to you about something important, nothing to do with your previous charges. Can we come inside?'

'I ain't done nothing wrong,' the voice said.

'We're not here to arrest you,' I assured him.

The door opened. After showing our identity badges, Angie and I were led into the front room.

Gary was about forty years old with short dark hair and a web with a spider tattooed on the side of his neck. Slivers of daylight entered the room through the gaps in the curtains and dust particles floated up in the air. The heavy smell of weed hung in the room. He pointed to a frayed two-seater settee, and Angie and I took a seat.

'Gary,' I said, 'we know you were in the old mobile office on the road to Coalville recently. Your DNA was found in a condom there. We need to ask you a few questions about what you were doing there.'

He looked at me, scratched a scab on his arm, then looked at Angie. 'I had sex, so what?'

'A man was murdered in the warehouse nearby. We just want to know if you saw or heard anything.'

Gary lit a cigarette and took a couple of long drags.

We waited.

'Well, you probably know I came out of the nick two, three weeks ago,' he said. 'I knew Tracey from before and saw her on the street a few nights ago, looking for punters. She needs money to feed her habit, like. I had —' he looked at us — 'something that could stop her from getting sick, you know, but she didn't have any money. Said she'd pay me later or she could pay me another way. Well, I ain't been with a woman for a while, being banged up and all. So we went to the hut.'

He took another long drag of the cigarette and flicked the ash into an overflowing ashtray.

'How did you get there? Did you drive?' asked Angie.

'Nah, don't have a car at the moment. I borrowed my son's electric scooter.'

I thought of how these scooters were now the preferred mode of transport by dealers on estates such as these. Or electric bikes with the false square bags of fast-food delivery companies hanging on the back.

'Anyway, we went into this disused office and started doing our thing when car headlights stopped nearby. I heard the car door open and a man shouted for someone to get out. Tracey told me to stay still. We heard a bloke screaming and Tracey were terrified. Then the headlights switched off. After a few minutes we got dressed and scarpered. I didn't see nothing out there.'

'What about Tracey? What's her second name? Where can we find her?'

'Trollope,' he replied.

Angie gave him a hard stare.

'That's her name. Tracey Trollope. She'll probably be trying for lunchtime trade. She's usually on the corner of North Street.'

The area around North Street was busy with traffic. I pulled up alongside the kerb and a woman with cropped, bleached-blonde hair wearing a short denim skirt and knee-length black boots leaned into the open passenger window, her hands placed on the car door. The first thing that struck me was the strong smell of cheap perfume; the second thing were the letters 'LOVE' tattooed between the joints of her pale fingers on one hand and 'HATE' on the other.

'Not done a sandwich for a while,' she said, looking at Angie and me. 'Could be your tasty filling?'

'You Tracey Trollope?' I asked.

She stood up and took two paces back. 'You the fuzz? I ain't done nothing wrong.'

'Well, soliciting for a start,' replied Angie. 'But relax, we're not here about that.'

'We've just seen your mate, Gary,' I said. 'He told us we'd find you here.'

'The dirty little snitch.'

'Tracey, relax,' I said. 'We want to talk to you about what you saw the other night. When you were with him.'

She scratched the needle marks on her arm. A red rash appeared where she scratched. 'Got nothing to say. Didn't see nothing.'

'Well, we could run you down to the station and have a chat about soliciting, or we could just have a chat somewhere quiet and then you can go,' said Angie.

I got out, pulled back the seat of my two-door Coupé and Tracey squeezed in behind me. I drove straight to the murder site and we led her to the derelict mobile office.

Tracey explained that she and Gary had arrived in the dark on the scooter, he'd parked it to the side away from the road so nobody could see it. 'There's a mattress on the floor under the window and while we were doing our thing, car headlights came up from behind. I told Gaz to be quiet and then I looked through the gap in the window. Two men were shouting at another guy to get out of the car. This other guy were Asian, like you, and his hands were tied behind his back. The Asian guy kept saying, "Please let me go, I'll give you a lot of money," but the other men were having none of it. One of them had a gun. The Asian guy started running and that's when I lost sight of them. Gaz and me got out fast.'

'What about the two men you saw with the Asian guy? Can you describe either of them?' asked Angie.

'One of them had short blond hair. The one with the gun. I think he was holding it in his left hand.'

'Can you recall anything else, Tracey? This is really important,' I said.

She closed her eyes for a moment. The nearby traffic noise was momentarily drowned out by the roar of an aircraft's engines taking off from East Midlands Airport. 'Yes, there is something else,' she said. 'The guy holding the gun had a tattoo on his arm. A circle with lines inside.'

We drove Tracey back to where we'd picked her up and said someone would be in touch to take a formal statement. As she climbed out of the car, I could see her hands were shaking and she was scratching at her arms.

As she walked back to her corner, I called her back. Took out my wallet and gave her forty pounds. 'Please buy some food with this. Call it loss of earnings for helping us. And thanks for your help.'

Tracey smiled gratefully, her pale blue eyeshadow glittering. 'Don't fancy being one of my regulars, d'you?'

'You know you're not supposed to give drug addicts money, don't you?' said Angie, as I turned the car around and pressed down on the accelerator.

CHAPTER 12

I had arranged a briefing session the next day so that the team could go through the evidence and help me formulate further lines of enquiry. Cynthia was no longer in Leicester so I arranged a video link with her from her office in London.

I sat at the head of the conference table, with Jamie and Angie sitting to my right and Tim to the left.

'Okay, this is what we've got so far,' I said. 'Sunil Kumar faked his own death on stage. He said, and I quote, it was 'wonderful publicity'. I think he may have done so to revitalise his flagging career, because he hadn't made a film for at least a couple of years. What he didn't know is that he'd been poisoned already and his time was up.

'*Question one*: Why was he killed? We know that our second victim, *The Turbanator* — or Ali as MI5 know him — killed Kumar. We are still working on that man's real identity but we know he was a Muslim, who most likely had plastic surgery to enable him to escape ready identification. We know from Tim and Cynthia he had connections with a drugs baron named Mohammed Jahangir in Pakistan. But why kill a Bollywood superstar?

'*Question two*: Why was *The Turbanator* killed? We think the symbol graffitied in the warehouse next to his body refers to a wealthy Arab extremist called Abdul Hussain, but what message is he sending?

'*Question three*: Who were the two men who took *The Turbanator* to the warehouse? One has been described as a white man with short blond hair and with possibly the same symbol tattooed on his arm. And what about his accomplice?

Who is he?'

'Please remember,' said Cynthia, from the laptop screen, 'the security services were monitoring our second victim's activities closely. He had recently arranged for a shipment of drugs from Pakistan to Isfahan in Iran. Isfahan contains a top-secret defence facility so we believe his activities would have got approval from the Iranian authorities. We do know that drugs that make it into Iran are then usually shipped southwest towards the Persian Gulf and are loaded onto ships, which make their way through the Red Sea into the Mediterranean. The dealers then distribute it — cut with other stuff, of course — throughout Europe.'

'But at the moment, Cynthia, we don't know how any of that links to our case,' said Tim.

Cynthia nodded. 'Perhaps he was killed for a drug deal gone wrong, and it had nothing to do with the death of Sunil Kumar, but that would seem to be too much of a coincidence. We are still trying to establish a link between Mr Kumar and "Ali".'

'And there's no intelligence to suggest Sunil was involved in the drug trade?' I asked.

'Nothing so far,' Cynthia replied.

'Do we know if any informers, either here in Leicester or anywhere else, know who *The Turbanator* is?' asked Angie. She turned to me. 'I'm assuming nobody's come forward, Sir?'

'Not yet, Angie. It would be good to formally identify him.'

There was an electronic ping and Angie looked at her own screen.

'Sir,' she said, 'you'll want to take a look at this. It's the CCTV footage from the airports that I requested. Shall we stream it onto the main screen?'

'Yes, please,' I said. 'Jamie, can you also send it to Cynthia?'

The footage started with scenes at Mumbai airport that were unremarkable. The Kumars were in the lounge while their luggage, consisting of four suitcases and two holdalls, was transported by an electronic buggy and placed in the open compartment under the fuselage of the plane.

The scenes from Dubai Airport were similar. The couple disembarked, the luggage was taken off by two luggage handlers and placed carefully onto the back of an electric trolley. Then the Kumars left the airport in a chauffeur-driven limousine. When the couple returned to board their flight to Prague, nothing untoward was shown on the footage.

The stream then switched to scenes of their plane coming in to land at Prague Airport. The images followed the couple strolling into the VIP lounge where Priyanka Kumar read a magazine while her husband spoke on the phone, and a member of staff served them refreshments. On the tarmac outside, the pilot oversaw the refuelling of the plane and stayed there until it had been completed. The door to the luggage compartment hung down, and the pilot climbed the few steps into the main body of the plane. While he was inside, a luggage trolley stacked with suitcases glided past, driven by a man who wore a peaked cap and dark glasses. As it travelled past, he tossed a medium-sized case deep into the luggage compartment of the plane. After a few minutes, the co-pilot appeared, secured the door to the luggage compartment and entered the plane.

'Pause it there, Jamie,' I said. 'Can you rewind and play the last couple of minutes again?'

Jamie complied.

We all watched as the suitcase was thrown into the plane's luggage compartment.

'That's odd,' I said. 'It doesn't look as if that piece of luggage was added to the plane through the correct channels. Possibly a link to our drug dealer? Angie, when we're done, please contact the head of security at Prague Airport, send them a copy of the image of the man driving that luggage trolley and ask if they can identify him.'

Angie nodded.

'We've got the contact details of the crew, including the pilot, haven't we?' I asked.

'Yes, but they're not in the UK anymore,' Angie replied. 'They weren't under suspicion so no one attempted to detain them.'

'It would be good to speak with the pilot,' I said. 'See whether he can throw any light on this.'

'We can get the pilot,' said Cynthia from the laptop. 'We'll ask the Indian government to send him here to help with our enquires. But he doesn't seem to be a witness to what's been thrown into the hold.'

'Let's continue and see what happens next,' I said.

The plane taxied along the runway at East Midlands Airport in the middle of the afternoon and came to a gentle halt near the main buildings. The couple alighted once the door was open and the luggage hold was opened by the pilot, while the rest of the crew entered the main terminal. Not long after the luggage hold was opened, a baggage handler arrived in an electronic buggy and unloaded four suitcases and two holdalls, placed them in the buggy and entered the main terminal. The cameras followed the buggy. There was no sign of the extra case thrown into the luggage hold.

'Pause the film, please,' I requested. 'Angie, have we got any other images of the plane while it's parked there?'

'No, Sir.'

'So, what happened to that extra case? Please get onto the

head of security at East Midlands and ask them for the footage from the camera monitoring the area around the plane.'

We waited for a few minutes while Angie spoke on the phone.

'They're working on it now, Sir. They'll get us the footage as soon as possible.'

I thanked her and asked Jamie to stream the footage of Mr and Mrs Kumar entering the Regency Hotel's main reception area. Despite it being a grey October afternoon, they were both wearing sunglasses. A concierge followed behind them with a trolley. The four suitcases were stacked on top of each other and a holdall was placed on top. As the guests signed in, the luggage was wheeled towards a service lift, presumably to be taken up to their suite.

'Wait a minute, Sir,' Angie said. 'What's happened to the second holdall?'

'What?' I asked.

'The second holdall. They had two holdalls at Mumbai Airport. But only one is visible at the hotel.'

We took another look at the video. The Kumars weren't carrying anything.

'Well spotted, Angie.'

'Yup,' said Tim, 'and the extra case is definitely missing.'

'It seems that the Kumars didn't know anything about that extra case,' I said, 'but we obviously need to ask Mrs Kumar about the second holdall.'

After a comfort break, Angie announced that the extra footage from East Midlands Airport had been sent over.

The images were grainy, but a man in a cap and overalls, who could have been a maintenance engineer, opened the luggage compartment of the plane and grabbed the extra suitcase. He hurried away out of camera shot, but another camera picked up a fuzzy figure with the case running towards a chain-link fence in the distance.

I asked Angie to pause the film and ring the security team at the airport again, ask if they could identify the individual as a matter of urgency. They said they would get back to her as soon as possible.

'The counter-terrorism team has been picking up a lot of chatter on the Dark Web that something big is being planned, possibly a terrorist attack,' Tim said. 'The East Midlands has been mentioned and I wonder if it has something to do with this case. A recurring message in various chat rooms is "Mission Accomplished" and "Present Delivered", but we had no idea before now what that referred to. The biggest fear now is that it could be about a bomb. What do you think, Cynthia?'

'We're trying to work out if there is a real threat and, if so, where it's aimed,' Cynthia replied. 'My Director General is very conscious of acting on every legitimate lead.'

'It's Diwali in a couple of days,' I said. 'That would be the perfect time for a terrorist group to make a statement. Cause maximum mayhem, get maximum publicity, especially if the target is here in Leicester. Maybe that's the link with Sunil Kumar's murder? The celebrations here are being targeted?'

'Maybe,' Cynthia said, 'but it's too soon to link them. We'll keep a close eye on the online chatter.'

Angie's phone rang.

'The security team at the airport say the man in the footage could be any one of their workers or engineers,' she relayed to us. 'They can't tell from the grainy footage. They'll try to get better images to see if they can identify him but it doesn't sound promising. One of their team went to the chain-link fence and found that a part of it had been snipped so it looks like the suitcase disappeared through there.'

I thanked all of them and closed the meeting. As they filed out the door, I asked Tim and Cynthia to speak to their teams, specifically whether they could pick up any intelligence regarding planned terrorist attacks during Diwali — in Leicester or anywhere else. Jamie returned to his team while Angie continued to make her phone calls and follow up any leads online.

I dialled Priyanka Kumar's mobile number. After the usual pleasantries, and an update on developments so far, I asked about the luggage she and her husband had brought with them to the UK.

She paused for a moment and then said, 'Oh, we had four suitcases, all leather of course, and two large holdalls, again both soft leather.'

'And did all of your luggage arrive with you at the Regency Hotel?'

'Yes ... I think so. Sorry, with everything else that's happened I don't remember much about the luggage.'

'Not at all. I know it's an odd question. Can I just confirm, though, that nothing was missing?'

'I unpacked the cases, then hung our clothes in the wardrobe. Oh, wait a minute, there was only one holdall when we arrived. I rang the hotel reception to ask where the second holdall was and they said they would look for it. They found it a few hours later. Apparently, our chauffeur didn't look carefully inside the boot of the car. There was no harm done. Why do you ask?'

'I just wanted to make sure everything was accounted for, Mrs Kumar. The CCTV images when you and your late husband checked in only showed one holdall, but we knew from the footage at the airport that there were two.'

'I see. Well, thank you for being so thorough, Inspector Sharma. I hope you are as diligent in tracking down my husband's killer as you are in spotting missing luggage. I want someone to pay for what has happened.'

After a few more pleasantries, we said goodbye. I drummed my fingers on the table, wondering if Mrs Kumar had been completely honest with me, or whether she knew something about that second holdall.

Angie looked up. I told her what Mrs Kumar had said and asked her to verify it with the hotel.

'The holdall was missing for a while, but it was eventually recovered, according to the hotel manager,' Angie told me after hanging up the phone. 'The chauffeur hadn't noticed it when the boot was unloaded. He drove back to his office, there was a phone call a couple of hours later from the hotel, the holdall was found and then returned. The hotel has given me the name of the chauffeur.'

'Please run a check on him, Angie. How long he's been working for the company, background, and so on.'

Angie did some quick checks online. 'Name's Brian Melbourne, Sir, age fifty-eight. He runs the car hire company with his younger brother, David. They specialise in luxury short-term hires — mostly by footballers, TV stars, and prominent local business people. The company was founded twenty-three years ago, all properly registered with Companies House. Online reviews are good.'

The chauffeur sounded bona fide but I still didn't like the fact that the holdall had gone missing for a few hours.

Angie's mobile rang. It was the head of security at East Midlands Airport. She put him on speaker and told him I was present.

'I'm sorry it's taken me a while to get back to you, Sergeant Deacon,' he said. 'We've taken a closer look at the images of the baggage handler and you'll be pleased to hear that we've been able to identify the man. His name is Christopher George. We only just hired him. He said he preferred to work lates or nights, which was music to the ears of the managers interviewing him.'

'And he worked the two o'clock till ten o'clock shift on that particular Thursday?' I asked.

'Yes, that's right.'

'Do you have a photograph of him for identification purposes?'

'Yes, all of our staff wear identity badges on their lanyards. I'll send a copy over to you now.'

A moment later, a photograph of a man who looked to be in his mid-thirties peered at me from my computer screen. Heavy set. Blue-grey eyes. Close-cropped blond hair.

'Anything else we should know about him?'

'Yes…' The head of security cleared his throat. 'He's disappeared. He hasn't turned up for any more shifts since that Thursday.'

'I see. Is there anything else you can tell me about him — any other identifying features, for example?'

'Well, one of our baggage handlers was with him before Mr Kumar's jet arrived. He said the guy had a tattoo on the inside of his arm.'

'Let me guess,' I said, 'a circle with lines within it and a lightning bolt going through it?'

'Yes, that's right,' he replied, surprised.

CHAPTER 13

Before finishing for the day, I asked Angie to circulate the image of Christopher George to all the usual channels — his name hadn't thrown up any hits and I was pretty sure it was a fake.

I left HQ some time later and went to the firearms range to practice my skills as I had recently trained as a firearms officer. I undertook basic gun training in the Met, but was now fully accredited and licensed to carry the usual handgun issued to firearms' officers, the Glock, along with the Heckler and Koch sub-machine gun. Afterwards, I drove home, turning left onto the Golden Mile on my way. Diwali was tomorrow and the brightly-lit saree shops were doing a brisk trade. The vegetarian restaurants, serving a variety of mouth-watering food, were busy with customers. The sweet marts, selling yellow *pendas*, chocolate *barfi*, *chevda*, and *jalebi* had long queues of people stretching out onto the pavement.

The heavy traffic crawled along the road. Despite the apparently happy atmosphere along the Golden Mile, there was undoubtedly tension in the air and on the streets. One of the shop windows was boarded up and shards of broken glass were being swept up and thrown into a skip. Groups of youths jostled past each other.

I tried not to think about what a bomb explosion could do to this area, my area, my spiritual and cultural home. It would be devastating.

A cold wind hit my neck as I stepped out of the car and walked to my front door. I stopped to say hello to my neighbours, an

Indian couple who lived a few doors down and who had previously looked after Fernando while I'd been on holiday. They had a young son who I was convinced had taught Fernando some unsavoury words while he stayed with them.

I unlocked my front door and stepped into the dark lounge. It was quiet. No welcome from Fernando. I turned on the light. His cage was empty. My heart raced. 'Fernando? Fernando! Where are you?' I shouted.

Nothing.

'Fernando?'

I ran up the stairs, shouting his name. I burst into the bedroom and saw him. He was lying on his back on the floor, his wings spread wide.

His eyes closed.

I ran to him and picked him up, staring into his face.

'Boo!' he squawked loudly, suddenly opening his big, round eyes.

'Fernando! Don't do that. I could've had a heart attack! I should slap you on the bum for scaring me like that.'

'Like Anita,' he replied.

'Fernando! Have you been watching us?'

He looked at me and blew a wolf whistle.

After changing, I decided to cook some dinner. I switched on the television for some background noise as I placed chicken kebabs in the hot oven. I looked at Fernando on his perch.

'I don't know why you're playing up, Fernando. You seem to have a contented life. You've got me, I look after you. And what do I have? Two kids I don't see enough of, and a lovely woman who lives on the other side of the country with a job which takes her all over the place.'

Fernando looked at me. I went to his cage and stroked his

head.

'I love you, Rohan.'

'I love you too, Fernando…'

But he wasn't listening to me anymore. He was staring at the television screen.

I picked up the remote control and turned up the volume.

'…*and in the newly opened Tropical Birds' Kingdom,*' the presenter of the local news station was saying, '*visitors enjoyed seeing a variety of bird species, including flamingos and African parrots…*'

I stared at the screen with Fernando.

'*The African grey parrots are especially popular because of their talkative nature. The Kingdom is proud of the fact that they have breeding pairs. Here, we see a mating pair enjoying each other's company…*'

Two African grey parrots nuzzled each other and the camera cut out before they were shown engaging in any embarrassing activities.

Fernando continued watching the screen long after the end of the news item.

'Oh, Fernando, please don't be sad.'

His head drooped.

'Anita will soon be here. The house won't seem so empty then. We can all have a good time together.'

He gave me the evil eye at the mention of her name, flipped around on his perch, and lifted his long, angular tail.

'No, Fernando, don't.'

He did.

After I finished eating and had washed up, I sat down and started watching some mindless soap opera on television. The room had warmed up, and I found it hard to keep my eyes open.

The sound of a firework whizzing outside my front window

startled me awake.

I looked at Fernando. 'Come on,' I said. 'Let's put you to bed. You want my earplugs?'

He stared at me, his body trembling. I knew the fireworks would only get worse.

'It's okay, Fernando,' I said, stroking the gossamer grey and white feathers on his head and neck. 'It's just people celebrating. Nobody's going to hurt you. But you may as well sleep in my room tonight. I'll bring the cage up for you.'

He jumped from his cage onto the thumb and forefinger of my hand. I placed him on top of the television set.

'Now don't mess the screen with anythi—'

A loud explosion shook the house. Fernando screeched. Jagged pieces of plaster from the ceiling missed my head and fell onto the floor. The lights flickered, switched off and came back on.

Fernando screeched again. I rushed to his cage, put him inside for his own safety, and then ran out of the front door.

CHAPTER 14

Outside on the street people were running in all directions. The bright blue lights of burglar alarms were flashing, their piercing sounds going off.

'They're killing us! They're killing us!' a young man shouted as he ran past me.

'Who?' I replied above the din.

'Them! The terrorists!'

I ran towards the site of the explosion, heading toward the flames which were shooting high into the night sky. Dirt and debris littered the street. A middle-aged woman lay sprawled on the ground, her white saree scorched. I put out the few remaining embers, helped her to stand, and passed her on to others to look after.

I carried on running. Thick acrid smoke filled the air, the smell of gunpowder making me cough. In the distance the wail of a fire engine rose above the shouting of frightened voices.

I found the site of the explosion. The street held lock-up garages and small industrial units. Now, broken and twisted black metal glowed in the firelight. Cars were scorched and badly damaged, metal panels dented, tyres burning. A small hatchback lay on its roof, most of the back missing.

'Is anyone hurt?' I shouted. 'Does anybody need help?'

I repeated the questions in Gujarati and Hindi, but no one answered. I coughed and bent over, as the smoke got into my lungs.

Two fire engines rushed past, followed closely by five ambulances.

The fire officers quickly got to work. While some sprayed the ferocious flames with water, others led people to safety. Another two fire engines appeared and cordons were quickly put in place.

A small crowd gathered to watch the fire officers deal with the blaze. The fire chief urged them to go home, as it was not clear what had caused the explosion or whether there would be another one. A few people dispersed, but most stayed. I grabbed the megaphone from the fire chief and implored the crowd to go home, to no avail.

Uniformed police officers soon appeared, some in protective riot gear, and moved the crowd back. Rumours quickly spread that a number of people had been killed in the explosion.

There was a tap on my back and I turned round.

'Tim! What are you doing here?' And then I realized the stupidity of my question given that he worked in counter-terrorism.

'Rohan, we need to clear the streets, quickly. We don't yet know what caused this. If it was a bomb, there could be another device ready to go off.'

Both he and I directed the uniforms to push the crowds back, and carried on urging the people to go home. Once things were under control, I got on the phone to the team at HQ to put out appeals on social media for information. I woke up Superintendent Breedon and asked him to make a statement saying that the situation was under control and a thorough investigation would be undertaken about what had happened.

The bomb disposal squad had arrived and was sweeping nearby streets and communal areas, while the forensics team scoured the ground. As the night progressed, the flames died down and steam rose from hot and twisted metal doused in water.

Tim Lafferty, Ben Carter and I stood on the corner, staring at the destruction in front of us.

'Any fatalities?' I asked Ben.

'Not that we know of but we'll know more soon from the hospital.'

'Do we know what caused the explosion?' Tim asked.

'Not yet,' replied Ben.

'No evidence of metal screws and bolts that could have been used in a bomb?' I asked.

'No, nothing we're aware of so far.'

I rang Angie and asked her to get hold of CCTV footage from the surrounding areas and to put out an appeal for dashcam footage from cars travelling in the area.

After the bomb disposal team and the fire chief had given us the all-clear, and while the forensics team carried out their painstaking examination of the scene on hands and knees, I dragged my weary body back home. The sun was just emerging on the horizon, the start of Diwali, the celebration of good over evil.

I entered my front room, opened Fernando's cage and spoke to him in a soothing manner. He was still trembling. I comforted him, tickled his midriff, until he nuzzled his head against my palm.

My mobile rang. The first question my mother asked me was if I was okay. She'd heard about the explosion on the local Asian radio station. 'Well, we all know who did it. But I'm glad you're safe.'

'Mum, nobody knows who is responsible yet.'

'It was a bomb. Everyone's saying it.'

I didn't say anything.

'And don't forget it's Diwali today,' she continued. 'So don't eat any lamb or chicken.'

I was tired. My body ached and I wanted to sleep.

'Why don't you come and see us today, Rohan? Have a bit to eat with us. It's an important day for us Hindus, after all.'

'Mum, I'm really sorry, but I've been up all night. I'm working on this case. There's just too much going on.'

'You're always too busy to come see me and your Dad, Rohan. Have you seen your children recently? Yasmin is out too much. She should have her head down doing homework, not thinking about anything else.'

'Such as what, Mum?'

'Well, you know, at that age the minds of both boys and girls tend to wander…'

'I'm sure nothing like that's going on.'

'And what about Karan? He's miserable all the time. He never speaks anymore.'

'Mum, both my children, your grandchildren, are better off with their mother. I see them as often as I can. They come to see you.'

'And what about your girlfriend? You've not brought her to meet us yet.'

'Anita is busy, she lives in the south and she travels all over the country.'

'Ah, well, at least she's an Indian, but it's a shame she can't speak Gujarati. She doesn't eat beef, does she?'

'No, Mum, she doesn't.'

I wasn't actually sure if that was true but I wasn't about to tell Mum that.

'Look, Mum, can we talk later? I've got to go.'

I asked her to pass on my love to Dad and ended the call. Not long after, Faye and my children rang, wanting to make sure I was all right. I wished all of them a happy Diwali and said I hoped to catch up with them soon.

I rang Anita and assured her that I was okay. She wanted to get straight in the car and come to see me but I managed to calm her down enough that she agreed to wait until the weekend.

Afterwards, I sipped *masala* tea in the silent gloom, trying to come to terms with some of the things my mother had said, worried about the prejudiced attitude she was displaying that I was sure was being echoed by many others in the community.

Fernando emerged slowly from his cage and started pacing up and down on the edge of the television set. He looked at me. I stared at the fraying edges of the carpet, trying hard not to be angry with my mother's attitude.

'Why are some people —'

'Nuts!' he squawked.

'Yes, nuts,' I replied.

I looked up at him.

He'd raised his left wing.

CHAPTER 15

When I woke up later in the day, the city was tense. Uniformed officers had been stationed in volatile areas to calm nervous residents. There had been isolated incidents between groups of youths, with reports of at least one stabbing. Journalists from national and local television stations were encouraging everyone they came across to talk to them and most people being interviewed spoke about their particular community being victimised. Youth workers and leaders of various community groups appealed for calm.

While all this was going on, my team were busy trying to identify the person who rented the lock-up garage where the bomb disposal team had confirmed the explosion had occurred.

'But there's no sign of any explosives, not the conventional sort,' said Tim, once I was back in the office.

Angie rushed into the room. 'Sir, we've found the guy who rented the lock-up garage.'

She sat down and explained that the man had been apprehended at Manchester Airport before he could board a flight to Dubai. He had confirmed his identity after a car's dashcam footage showed him leaving the garage. Our colleagues in Manchester were already bringing him down to us and would be here within the hour.

A little while later, Tim, Angie and I entered the interview room. The tape recorder was switched on and the camera started recording. Tim and I sat opposite the suspect, while Angie took a chair in the corner. I read him his rights and explained the procedure to him. We had arranged for a solicitor to represent him.

'You are Mr Cyril Braganza,' I said, 'and you are twenty-three years old. Is that correct?'

'Yes, Sir.' There was black stubble on his cheeks. His eyes were shifty, nervous.

'I understand that you came to this country from Goa, in India, eighteen months ago to study computer science at the university as a post-graduate student. Is that correct?' I continued.

'Yes, Sir.' He clasped and unclasped his hands. 'Please, Sir, I didn't mean to harm anyone.' His eyes darted from left to right. He looked terrified.

'Why were you storing explosives in the lock-up garage?' I asked.

'They were not explosives.' He turned to look at his solicitor.

'You don't have to say anything if you don't want to,' the solicitor advised.

Cyril Braganza pursed his thin lips and nodded. He turned back to me. 'Sir,' he continued, 'I came from Goa to study on a student visa. My father thought it was God's wish for me to come here. But the fees are very expensive, more than twenty thousand pounds a year. And I also need somewhere to stay, food to eat. My father has a small farming plot in southern Goa and he borrowed money against it to send me here to study.

'Mr Sharma, Sir, I'm a poor Roman Catholic man from Goa. Not a Hindu. Not a Muslim. I came here to study. But after my first year at university, I was having less and less money. I couldn't pay my rent. Sometimes I had to use candles because I didn't have enough money to put in the electric meter. I couldn't ask my father or anybody else for money. Life became very hard. It was not what I thought it would be.' Tears filled his eyes. He paused. 'I could see other people in the area struggling with their bills too. No heating. No electricity. Then I found a man who was selling gas cylinders for heaters and for people to use on iron gas rings at home. You know, the gas rings used to cook and heat food at wedding receptions. This was cheaper than using the gas from the gas companies. I thought this was a good way of earning some money and keeping my room warm. I could also cook my own food.'

'So you stored these highly dangerous cylinders in the lock-up garage in a built-up area?' I asked.

'Mr Sharma, Sir, I know it was wrong, but I was desperate. And I was also helping some very poor people.'

'How many cylinders were there?' I asked.

'About twenty.'

'Why did they explode?'

'I don't know, Sir. Perhaps there was a leak in one of the cylinders? Someone throws a lighted cigarette end nearby...' He tugged at the collar of his dark fleece. 'I also stored fireworks there. I was selling them cheap for Diwali. I bought them from a dealer here. He got them from China. Their fireworks are much better, more powerful than the ones you can buy here.'

'But not subject to proper health and safety standards,' said Tim.

Cyril Braganza did not respond.

I stared at him and clenched my fists under the table, thinking of the stupidity of his actions. The smell of gunpowder on the night of the explosion made sense now.

'After the explosion, why did you run away? Why were you about to fly to Dubai? Have you got contacts there?' I asked.

'Sir, my father will lose his land because of me. We have owned our family farm for many generations. I know I did wrong. I wanted to go back home. Not end up in prison here. I had just enough money to get to Dubai. I have an Indian passport and visa to go there. It wouldn't be a problem.'

'And what about all the lives you've ruined here? The damage you've caused?' I asked.

He looked at me across the desk. A tear ran down his cheek. 'Sharma *Sahib*, please don't tell my father what I've done. It'll ruin him.'

'Cyril, it's not up to us to tell him. I'll let you do that. For now, we're going to charge you with causing an explosion which endangered life and property. And once you have served your sentence, you'll be deported.'

I asked Angie to finish the interview and to start the process for the initial charges.

In the corridor outside, I asked Tim, 'What d'you think of him?'

'Doesn't fit the profile for our case. He's not a Hindu or a Muslim. He's not been on our radar at the CT unit. His story sounds plausible.'

'Yeah, it does. I'll ask the Indian Embassy in Birmingham to provide us with details about his family. He could be telling us the truth, but I'm not ruling him out just yet.'

CHAPTER 16

I spent early Saturday evening with my kids before Anita was due to arrive. We'd been to see the latest Avengers' film at the local cinema complex. Yasmin tolerated such films because of her brother, while I was just happy to spend time with them both. Now we were sitting in a busy pizza restaurant. Sadly, my children's taste in food was quite narrow. A side of chips with everything, definitely 'nothing ethnic' as Karan once said to me, although Yasmin was becoming more adventurous.

We were sitting at a quiet table in a corner but the restaurant was busy with other patrons. The loud voices of orders being shouted to the kitchen staff, who pulled dough and placed the stretched pizza bases in the open ovens, competed with the piped music coming from small, round speakers in the ceiling. Many of the customers were enjoying a good evening out.

'Did you enjoy the film, Karan?' I asked.

'Was all right,' he said with a shrug.

'That's the most you'll get out of him,' said Yasmin. 'He doesn't speak these days.'

He nudged her in the midriff with his elbow and she pushed him back. I asked them to stop it and to order their food.

Karan ordered a deep pan pizza, no salad, while I was surprised by my daughter's order of a Chicken Caesar salad with the dressing on the side and no chips. 'Because I'm watching my weight and don't want to get fat,' she pronounced, loudly.

'She's having a go at me, Dad, 'cos I'm fat.'

'Oh, Karan, you're not fat,' I said. 'Anyway, you're growing and it'll all change soon.'

'Not the way he eats,' said Yasmin.

'All the kids at school make fun of me anyway. I don't care.'

'Just ignore them. Please don't make yourself miserable,' I said.

A teenage boy of about sixteen entered the restaurant and walked past our table. He smiled at Yasmin. There was no doubt my daughter, with her olive skin and glossy dark hair, was turning into an attractive young woman. The braces on her teeth were long gone and there was a hint of make-up on her face.

Karan registered what was going on and said, 'She has a boyfriend.'

'Have you, darling?' I asked Yasmin.

'Oh, he's just a friend. He's called Peter.'

'Does your Mum know about him?'

'Yes, she does.'

'Well, you be careful. Don't go doing anything silly.'

'Dad! He's just a friend. We do homework in the library after school.'

'Okay, darling, as long as you're happy,' I said, dropping the subject because I didn't want to alienate her.

'Anyway,' Yasmin said, 'we don't know what *you* get up to with Anita.'

I raised an eyebrow. 'Not a lot, Yasmin. We live miles away from each other.'

'I'm happy you're happy, Dad,' she said. 'We both are. You need someone else in your life.'

The food arrived and we ate in silence for a while.

'What about what's going on, Dad?' said Yasmin, after a while. 'All the kids at my school know you're involved in what's going on, but they never see you on the telly.'

I put my knife and fork down. 'My superiors know more

about the case than I do,' I said. 'That's why they're on the telly to explain things, to calm people down.'

'But they never mention all the work you do, Dad. They never mention your name,' Yasmin persisted.

'Oh, it's just how it is. Please don't worry too much about it.'

Yasmin stood up, saying she needed to go to the toilet.

'Don't go talking to any strange boys,' I said.

As I turned, I saw Karan's deeply unhappy face across the table from me. I reached out, touched his hand and asked if he was all right. He shrugged.

'Come on, Karan. Please tell me. I'm your dad after all.'

He stopped slurping his fizzy drink, put the large glass down, stared at me, and then burst into tears.

I hopped round to the other side of the table and put my arms around him.

'Dad, I'm so unhappy. Nobody wants me. Nobody loves me. Yasmin's got a boyfriend. Mum and Pierre are always together.'

'Oh, Karan,' I said, squeezing him tight. 'I love you, and I'll always be here for you.'

He turned his face and looked up at me. 'But you're not, are you? Your work keeps you busy. You're now with Anita. You see more of her than you do of me and Yasmin.'

'I'm sorry, but I am here now.' His comments cut deep. And he was right, of course. 'Why don't you come and stay with me sometimes? Just you and me.'

He didn't answer.

After a while, he said, 'And the kids at school call me names. Not just because I'm fat. The white kids make fun of me because of my colour. And some of the Asian kids say I'm not one of them because I can't speak any of their languages.' He started sobbing again.

Yasmin interrupted us. I hadn't seen her coming back. She

sat in the seat I had vacated and didn't say anything. I tried to cheer us all up by asking what they wanted for dessert.

The tension subsided and I felt slightly better about things by the time I'd dropped them back home, though I was determined to make sure I spent some quality time with Karan.

As I entered the front room of my house, Fernando blew a wolf whistle and then squawked, 'There once was a girl from Nantucket.'

'Fernando, please, no dirty limericks tonight. I'm not in the mood. Who on earth taught you that one anyway?'

His round grey eyes looked at me. He scratched the side of his head with a claw.

'Spoilsport,' I heard, as I asked the smart speaker to play George Michael's greatest hits.

My phone pinged. I looked at the message that had come through.

If you want to know more about why Sunil Kumar was killed meet me tonight at 11 o'clock at the warehouse. Don't tell any of your colleagues. If you do, or if I spot anyone following you, I will not come.

I closed the message. The soaring, emotive voice of George Michael filled the room as he sang about a careless whisper.

CHAPTER 17

It was ten minutes past eleven when I drove into the deserted industrial estate. The faint lights from passing car headlights illuminated my trashed surroundings for a few seconds and then it all was dark again. The forensics team had swept the area for any evidence and it had been returned to its natural, dilapidated state. I walked into the warehouse where *The Turbanator*'s body had been found. Heavy footsteps behind me. My body tensed as I turned round.

'Saw you come in, Mr Sharma,' said a deep, male voice. The silhouette of a tall figure stopped a couple of metres from me.

Only then did I realise the stupidity of my actions. The man was now blocking my exit. And in my rush to make the appointment, I hadn't informed anyone where I was.

'Who are you,' I asked in a calm voice, trying to control the rate of my breathing. 'Why did you want to meet me here?'

'Thought it was a suitable place, what with what happened over there.' He indicated the wooden beam with a wave of his hand. 'And it's secluded — I didn't want us to be disturbed.'

The man stepped forward out of the shadow. He was dressed in black jeans, a black polo-neck sweater and had a shiny black balaclava mask over his face. Only his eyes and lips were visible.

'I don't have time to play games,' I said. 'If you've got any information for me about the killing of Sunil Kumar, then shoot.' I immediately regretted my choice of words.

'Not the phrase I would've used,' the man said, 'but I think it's important you know what you're dealing with.'

'Who are you?' I asked again.

'Let's see. Call me Shah. Duleep Shah. The first name can be use by a Sikh and, as you know, Shah is a Muslim or Hindu name.'

'Okay, fine. That makes you a citizen of the world. I'm sorry, but I don't have time for this,' I said. 'I'm leaving.' I started towards the door.

He took a step in front of me. 'Listen to me. You have to understand community politics here in Leicester. Your white colleagues in the counter-terrorism unit are fed all sorts of rubbish by their informants and they believe it hook, line and sinker.'

'And I'm sure they check it out alongside other evidence.'

'As I was saying,' the man growled, 'they believe it because they don't understand community dynamics. They don't understand the importance of family honour, both among the Hindus and among the Muslims. They don't understand how powerful women are in individual families. All they see is the *burka* and women in sarees walking behind their husbands.'

'Thank you for the sociology lesson. Who exactly are you?'

'I'm part of a Hindu group that monitors the activities of prominent individuals — politicians, business people, celebrities — and look for those who subvert our way of life. Or the way Hindus are meant to live: not eating beef, not drinking alcohol, maintaining family honour —'

'Does that include engaging in various forms of abuse behind closed doors?' I asked.

'There are,' he continued, ignoring my question, 'people who undermine their own religion and culture. People like Sunil Kumar. People like him are a law unto themselves. They pollute the minds of the young with their loose morals.'

'So, you belong to a Hindu group that's monitoring the activities of a prominent Hindu star?'

'The point I'm making is that things are not what they seem. Sunil Kumar was involved in all sorts of shady activities, but we have no incriminating evidence. You need to look into his life, his personal life, his life in India.'

'Sorry, I'm only interested in what I can investigate in this country. The rest is beyond my jurisdiction... What about the guy in the turban? Who was he and why did he kill Mr Kumar?'

The man didn't reply.

'Do the letters *A* and *H* mean anything to you?' I asked.

'No, why d'you ask?'

I didn't answer.

'As I said to you, Mr Sharma, you need to broaden your mind and your investigation. It would also be good idea if you if you too acted more like a proper Hindu. You'll live a longer and much better life that way.'

'Is that a threat?'

He took a step back and melted into the night.

I took a deep breath, my thumping heart slowly returned to normal.

I got home long past midnight and flopped into bed, half undressed. I was shattered from the events of the last few nights and hadn't had much sleep, but I still had a restless night. I was woken up at seven by my phone ringing.

'Sir,' said Angie, 'sorry to disturb you so early. But Cyril Braganza, the student from Goa? He's been found dead in his cell at Leicester Prison. I'm on my way there now.'

'Thanks for letting me know, Angie,' I said, jumping out of bed. 'I'll meet you there.'

I quickly rang Anita. It wouldn't be fair for her to drive to Leicester just for me to be working all day. She was disappointed, but she understood. She agreed to hold off until her job in the north started in a few days.

I was in the car within fifteen minutes and I opened the window to get some fresh air, to make sure I didn't fall asleep. The bright lights of the streetlamps reflected on the long bonnet of my car as it raced on the mainly empty roads towards the prison. The castle-like building on Welford Road, with its red brick walls thirty feet high, had a brooding presence, reflecting its history as a place of execution. Today, it held remand prisoners while they awaited trial in the courts.

After going through all the security measures, Angie, the prison governor and I stood on the upper landing of one of the wings, with rows of cells on either side. A blue forensic tent had been erected outside the door to one of the cells and wide-eyed inmates peered silently through their cell doors. Ben Carter and his team of forensic officers were already brushing dust, fibres and other materials into plastic evidence bags. I asked for two forensic suits from one of Ben's team and entered the cell, followed by Angie.

Nasreen was already inside. She smiled and said a formal, 'Good morning, Inspector Sharma.' She nodded to Angie. The body of Cyril Braganza hung from the bunkbed. He was naked from the waist down and the leg of one of his tracksuit bottoms was tied tightly around his neck. The other end was tied around the metal railing of the top bunk. His head was at an awkward angle and his open, lifeless eyes stared at the floor. He wore a stained grey T-shirt, his arms hanging loose by his sides.

'It seems he died several hours ago,' said Nasreen. 'The ambient temperature is still well below the body temperature, so the body is still cooling down. Death by strangulation is the most likely cause. I'm not sure I can tell you any more at this stage.'

'Any sign of foul play? Or was it self-inflicted?' I asked.

'I'll be checking for strangulation marks from a perpetrator and any other violent signs, but we are assuming suicide at the moment.'

'We've collected all the forensics we're likely to need,' said Ben, walking over. 'Got dust fibres, cotton fibres, fingerprints, and so on. Nothing obviously suspicious so far, but I'll confirm with you when we have analysed the results.'

Angie and I went outside and accompanied the prison governor to his office.

'Who found Mr Braganza, Sir?' Angie asked him.

'The officer on night duty,' replied the governor in a clipped military accent. 'Bharat Mistry. Neither he nor the other staff on duty saw or heard anything suspicious. He sounded reveille at six o'clock this morning, but there was no response from Mr Braganza, so he opened his cell and that's when he found him.'

'Is it usual to have only one prisoner in a cell?' I asked.

'Not unusual. There was another prisoner with Mr Braganza, hence the double bunk, but he was transferred to Gartree Prison yesterday afternoon.'

'Was Mr Braganza known to be suicidal at all?'

'No, not that we were aware of. He obviously wasn't happy to be here. Nobody is. But he got on with the other prisoners and was obedient when my officers asked him to do anything. We did not have him classified him as vulnerable.'

'Can we have the names and addresses of all the staff and prisoners who were here last night please?' asked Angie. 'Including the prisoner who recently shared the same cell.'

'You do realise that's hundreds of names, don't you?'

She smiled at him. 'Oh, and we need to interview Officer Mistry,' she continued, 'and all the staff who came into contact with Mr Braganza yesterday and this morning.'

The governor said he'd organise everything.

I drove the short distance to police HQ. As I did so, I placed a call. Meena Patel, the attaché at the Indian consulate in Birmingham, answered the phone.

'Good morning, Meena,' I said. 'Do you recall I got in touch recently regarding a man named Cyril Braganza? He was arrested for causing the explosion in Leicester.'

'I do, why?'

'Well, he's been found dead in his cell at Leicester Prison,' I told her.

'What?' She sounded shocked.

'It looks like a suicide, but I'm not ruling out foul play just yet. Did you find anything about his family background?'

'Look, Rohan, I think it's a good idea if you and I discuss this in person. I need to come to Leicester later today. How about we meet up then?'

We agreed a time and place.

I entered the incident room at police HQ and was surprised to find Tim and Cynthia already there. I briefed them on the latest development.

'Thanks, Rohan,' said Cynthia. 'We already heard about Braganza; that's why I'm here.'

'Let's see what Angie finds out,' Tim said. 'See if there's anything — or anyone — suspicious that comes up or if it's a straightforward case of suicide.'

'There's nothing straightforward about suicide,' I replied. 'Think of his family.'

He raised both palms, facing me. 'Fair point,' he said.

'Oh, by the way, Rohan,' said Cynthia, 'be careful what you say to Meena Patel — she isn't all she appears to be.'

I frowned. 'What do you mean? How d'you know about Meena? Or that I've been talking to her?'

'She's new on the scene, posted here from Nigeria. Prior to that she was in Bali. She's an expert on Islamic extremism and works as an agent for "RAW", the Research and Air Wing of the Indian government. We've been monitoring her movements and her communications. A recording of her conversation with you just now was sent to me on my phone.'

I stared at her.

'All the agencies do it,' continued Cynthia. 'They do it to us. We do it to them. It's the name of the game.'

'Are you monitoring my phone, too?'

She shrugged. 'Above my pay scale, Rohan.'

How the hell did I get involved in such a murky world? What else were they monitoring? I tried not to think too much about that.

The steady drumbeat of paranoia was already beating deep within me.

'Why would an agent from the Indian security service be interested in me?' I asked.

'Your role in the Sunil Kumar case makes you an ideal candidate to be monitored by RAW,' Cynthia replied. 'They may not trust the information about the case they're being given through official channels, so they are looking for someone on the inside to give them more. What we do know is that RAW is tracking the movements of Pakistani agents in this country, keeping tabs on their informants, their contacts. Most of the Indian and Pakistani agents who are over here we know about. We monitor their activities, they monitor ours, we know what they're doing, they know what we're doing; it's a real game of cat and mouse. Some are double agents, and they become our informers. It's a dangerous game and the stakes are high if they get caught.'

'So how does this link to Sunil Kumar?' I asked.

'We're not sure of his role yet,' said Cynthia. 'All we know is that his killer was working closely with the drug baron Mohammed Jahangir and Jahangir has links with the Pakistani secret service, and may even have been one of their agents at one time. And, as we know, ISI has strong links to fundamentalist groups like ISIL, ISIS and Al-Qaeda.'

'Wait a minute, Cynthia,' I said. 'ISI?'

'Yes,' she replied. 'It stands for Inter-Services Intelligence. The name refers to the fact that the Pakistani agents are serving officers from all three branches of the armed forces. Army, navy and air force.'

'I-S-I...' I said slowly, repeating each letter. 'When I asked Sunil Kumar at the hospital if he had any idea how he came to be poisoned, he said what sounded like "Eye Says." I thought he was referring to ISIS, but he could have meant ISI.'

'It's more likely he was referring to ISI than ISIS,' said Cynthia. 'There's a link there, given what we know about his killer. But why kill Kumar? What was the motive?'

'The drugs link is the most obvious one, isn't it?' said Tim. 'Kumar travels all over the world, often in private, chartered jets. He could've transported drugs fairly easily. It could explain the mystery of the missing suitcase from East Midlands Airport.'

'But would the Pakistani secret service be interested in something as banal — harmful as it is across the world — as the selling of heroin from the poppy fields of Afghanistan?' I asked.

Cynthia shrugged.

'What about the white guy who killed *The Turbanator* — the one with the tattoo who'd been working as a baggage handler at East Midlands Airport? Who do we think he is?' asked Tim.

'We don't know,' said Cynthia. 'Christopher George is coming up as a false name. From the addition of the graffitied symbol found in the warehouse next to the body, we think he has links with the Arab extremist Abdul Hussain, but apart from that nobody in MI5 or MI6 knows anything about him.'

'Is George actually Caucasian?' I asked. 'Many people in northern Pakistan and from large parts of the Middle East could be mistaken for Caucasian, especially if they've dyed their hair blond. Or if they're the children or grandchildren of the Russian soldiers who invaded Afghanistan in the 1980s and settled down with Afghan wives.'

'That's something to think about,' said Tim.

'I need time to process this. Things just don't seem clear to me anymore, if they ever were,' I said.

'Welcome to the world of espionage, Rohan,' said Cynthia. 'I deal with shadows all the time. They come alive, and then disappear back into the darkness as quickly as they appeared.'

CHAPTER 18

After finishing my meeting with Tim and Cynthia, I drove across the city to meet Meena Patel. The grey, drizzly streets were busy in the middle of the day. The city was gradually returning to normal after the disturbances leading up to Diwali, a tense and uneasy alliance between the various groups. I turned left at the large roundabout and along the Golden Mile. The devastation of the recent explosion was still evident with boarded-up windows, partly-standing walls and the destroyed lock-ups. The buildings would soon be mended and the windows replaced, unlike the fragile fabric of a community that was in danger of tearing itself apart.

Meena was already at The Omar Khayyam Persian restaurant when I got there. She was sitting at a quiet window table towards the back. After the usual pleasantries, we sipped chilled rose water while we decided what to eat.

'So, what brings you to Leicester, Meena?' I asked.

'Nothing to do with work, Rohan. It's my day off. Leicester has some of the best saree and jewellery shops in the UK. I come here for shopping now and again.'

'So, what can you tell me about Cyril Braganza and his family?' I asked. 'You sounded anxious to speak with me in person when we were on the phone earlier.'

She put her glass down. 'There's not a lot to tell really, but I thought it'd be good to meet you in person. It seems Cyril was who he says he was. His father owns a small plot of land in Goa. It's mortgaged and the funds were used to pay for Cyril's travel and studies here. They seem to have miscalculated how much it would all cost. This country is very expensive to live in, as you know. So Cyril started selling things on the side. There is no evidence linking him to any terrorist activities.'

She ran a finger round the rim of her glass. Her pale pink nail varnish glistened in the soft light.

'Tell me something,' I said. 'How does a cultural attaché like yourself — dealing in visas and other such matters — suddenly start talking about terrorist activities? Were you just dealing with visas when you were in Nigeria and Bali?'

Her finger paused on the edge of the glass rim. She looked at me. 'Well, you have done your homework, Inspector Sharma.'

'What exactly is your role, Meena? I know you work for RAW. I have my own sources too.'

'Ah, Mr Rohan, how good to see you,' interrupted Mr Rahimi, the Iranian owner of the restaurant, as he walked towards us with a beaming smile. 'And your pretty friend here. We don't often see you at lunchtime.'

I shook his hand warmly and introduced him to Meena. After a few more pleasantries, we ordered a light meal, almond salad and pitta bread for me, and a rice salad for Meena.

'Is Meena your real name?' I asked when Mr Rahimi had left.

'Meena, Geeta, Reena, Tina, what does it matter?'

'Rohan *is* my real name,' I said. 'It matters to me. You can go look it up in all the official documents if you haven't done so already. You might want to start with the Electoral Roll. It's open to all.'

She paused, then looked at me.

'Espionage is a dishonourable game played by honourable people,' she said. 'Or it's an honourable game played by dishonourable people. Take your pick. I like to think I'm in the former camp. It is one of the oldest professions in the world. You only have to think of the story of the Trojan horse to know how far back it goes.'

'If you're not going to be candid with me then there's no point in the British police, of which I'm one, liaising with you or any other representative of the Indian government.'

She tucked a strand of her hair behind her ear. A dangling gold earring twinkled. 'I really can't say very much to you, Rohan. The information about Cyril Braganza and his family is true. If he was involved in anything else, we're not aware of it.'

'I met a Hindu nationalist the other day. He told me to look into the personal life of Sunil Kumar. We haven't detected anything untoward, but I'm not in India and I don't have access to the information you have.'

Meena didn't say anything for a while. She stared at the traffic passing by on the road. 'I can tell you,' she said eventually, lowering her voice, 'that we've been monitoring Kumar's activities for a while. Kumar was very secretive, but we know for a fact he was involved in drug trafficking.'

'He was?' I asked in surprise. 'Well, that helps explain a few things.'

Meena raised an eyebrow but I didn't elaborate further. 'He had links to the Indian mafia,' she continued. 'It didn't surprise us that he stopped off in Dubai on his way here. He probably had a haul of heroin in his private jet. But we have no jurisdiction there or here. Over the years he has made millions, and paid off politicians and police officers, not only in India but around the world. He had protection in high places.'

'But not in Leicester,' I said.

'No, not in Leicester,' she said. 'We didn't think anything would happen to him here. And obviously neither did he. Given his fame and his money and his contacts, he thought he was untouchable.'

'So who is responsible for his death?' I asked. 'Someone involved in the drug trade?'

Meena shrugged. 'Your guess is as good as mine. I've told you all I know.'

'What about the man in the turban who killed him? We know he was involved in the drug trade in the Middle East and on the Indian sub-continent. Did they work together?'

'We have a pretty good profile on him. We — I mean RAW — agree with MI5 that the symbols found next to his body refer to Abdul Hussain. Hussain's group has been involved in atrocities all over the world and that symbol has appeared in areas where they've been active. But we don't yet know how Hussain or the man in the turban or Sunil Kumar are connected.'

'Welcome home, Rohan. Welcome!' squawked Fernando, as I stepped into the front room. He was excited to see me. He flew in and out of his cage, sat on the edge of the settee and then perched on the television screen.

'Nuts! Nuts!' he squawked.

'Yes, the world is nuts, Fernando. How're you?' I said, stroking his head.

He raised his left wing and I flicked a peanut at him. He flew into the air and grabbed it. I made a cup of *masala* tea, with cardamom, cinnamon and cloves. I sat down and drank it slowly.

'You've probably guessed Anita's coming to visit soon, Fernando. Well, I've been thinking —'

'Nuts!' he squawked.

'I've got a plan for you.'

I thought about his reaction when the news report about the Tropical Birds' Kingdom had been on. 'It's not fair you being here on your own while I'm working all the time. You need company.'

He stared at me.

'We'll discuss this later,' I told him.

I rang my mother and father and caught up with my children, who had just arrived home from school. Yasmin was upbeat, already thinking about Christmas and what she'd like to do, while Karan was still subdued. I tried to arrange a day when he and I could do something together but he was not forthcoming.

It was already dark when I rang off so I decided to cook spaghetti Bolognese, with some lamb mince and diced mushrooms. I ate it in front of a mindless gameshow on television, and then trudged upstairs at about ten. I hadn't drawn the curtains and car headlights lit up the room now and again. My eyelids were heavy.

My mobile rang and I woke with a start. The bedside clock told me it was almost midnight.

'Sir,' said Angie. 'We've got another body. I'm on my way to the location now.'

CHAPTER 19

The stars were embroidered on a deep, black velvet sky, while the bright, orange moon, like an early Christmas bauble, was large and full. I swung my Mercedes through the iron gates of the sprawling leisure park near the main road to the east of the city, waving to a uniformed officer stationed there. The tarmac road glistened under the streetlights as I parked up next to a number of police cars and a forensic van in the small car park. Fallen leaves swirled in the cold wind as I made my way towards six bright arc lights in the distance, behind a canopy of oak and silver birch trees. I pulled up the collar of my winter coat and walked briskly. A small animal rustled near the overflowing litter bins.

The children's adventure playground had been cordoned off with blue and white scene-of-crime tape, and windbreakers and canopies had been put up to prevent long-distance camera shots from social media ghouls. The arc lights, powered by portable, clacking generators, bathed the area in white. Scene of crime officers were busy at work, the flashgun of high-powered cameras going off periodically, and the quiet whirring of drone engines above, recording a bird's eye view of the scene.

I nodded to Ben Carter, as he directed the work of his team. Angie walked towards me, already wearing a white forensic suit. I could see the prone body in the distance.

'Good evening, Angie,' I said, as I donned the forensic suit offered to me and zipped it up.

'Good evening, Sir. By the way, I asked DI Lafferty to attend as well but, unfortunately, there's some sort of medical emergency with his wife's pregnancy. He and his wife are both at the hospital.'

I nodded, hoping it wasn't too serious. I'd catch up with Tim tomorrow.

I lifted the blue and white tape and we walked through the playground, past intricate wooden climbing frames, a seesaw, and a play ship.

I stared. Lying spread-eagled on top of the roundabout — which was shaped like a giant wooden ship's wheel — was a man. His lower back rested in the middle, his arms and legs stretched out as far as they would go. He was smartly dressed in a black leather jacket, white T-shirt and navy jeans with a dark leather belt. The black and grey stubble on his face indicated he had not shaved for a while. His brown lifeless eyes stared up at the stars, a pool of congealing blood on the ground below his head. The nails on his fingers were well-manicured and not those of a manual worker. The way his arms and legs were positioned reminded me of Leonardo da Vinci's Vitruvian Man.

Nasreen Khan was bent over the body, examining it with a magnifying glass, making a voice recording of her findings into a Dictaphone. She straightened up and walked towards me and Angie.

'Good evening, Inspector,' she said.

'Evening, Nasreen. What've we got?' I asked.

'Middle-aged man, looks Middle Eastern, not been dead very long — a couple of hours, maybe. The body's still warm but cooling rapidly. Some blood is still wet around the wound.'

'Cause of death?'

'Oh, that's easy. Shot in the back of the head. Once. With a soft-nosed bullet. That's why there's no exit wound at the front or side. Wouldn't have known what hit him. Instant death.'

'Anything to identify him?'

'Nope.'

'Any tattoos?'

'None that I've seen so far.'

'Thanks, Nasreen.'

The pathologist walked away.

'By the way, Sir,' Angie said, 'Cyril Braganza's death has been confirmed as suicide. The interviews we conducted at the prison didn't raise anything suspicious.'

'Thanks, Angie.' I called Ben Carter over. 'Ben, get the photographs of the victim's face, fingerprints and DNA processed as soon possible, please. Let's see if he's on our databases. Any signs or symbols near the body that you've seen?'

'No, Sir, nothing,' he said.

He turned to go when I spotted something.

'What's that long iron rod under the roundabout?' I asked. We both stared at the rod. It was about three metres long, bent at a right angle at one end. It looked like the shape of a starting handle to crank the engine of an old car. This rod was much longer though.

'Not sure, Sir. It was already here when we arrived.'

I thanked him. 'Who found the body, Angie?'

'The park supervisor over there, Sir. He's being comforted by one of the DCs. Says he's never seen anything like this before. Certainly not in a children's playground.'

'Let's go speak to him,' I said. 'Why don't you lead on the questioning? I'll chip in if necessary.'

After introducing me to Nick Buckley, Angie asked him when he discovered the body. He said he was getting ready to shut the park gates when he went towards the adventure playground.

'I could a see shape on the ship's wheel. At first, I thought it was a drunk sleeping it off. I shone my light on his face and was about to shake him when I saw his eyes.' He shuddered. 'Reminded me of the shining eyes of a dead fish. Then I saw the blood. It scared the hell out of me.'

'Did you see anything suspicious, Mr Buckley? Anyone nearby? Or hear anything?' asked Angie.

'No, Miss — sorry, Officer — nothing at all. Cars had all gone.'

'Lots of local families with their children use this park, don't they?' Angie asked.

'Yup, it gets very busy during the day with young mums and small children. Even in this cold weather. Gives them something to do. It's the only green space for miles.'

'What about the long metal rod under the roundabout? Any idea where that came from?'

The park supervisor shook his head. 'No, sorry. Anybody could've put it there. All I know is it weren't there when I arrived in the late afternoon. It's a funny thing to leave.'

'Any CCTV cameras anywhere?' continued Angie.

'Funny you should say that, Officer. We have cameras near the front gates, but they got vandalised a few weeks ago. Some teenager with an air pistol. But,' he continued, 'the council put new ones up, only a couple of days ago. They are in a new location, though, hidden behind a tree trunk near the gates. We've not had time to put up signs like we're meant to do, warning people they're being recorded.'

Angie and I smiled at each other, hopeful the footage would show something.

Angie took his details and those of the security firm that owned the cameras, said we'd make contact again for a full statement and let him go home.

'Well done, Angie. Great work.'

She beamed, her blue eyes intense in the white light.

'Please get the CCTV images from the security firm,' I instructed her. 'And tomorrow, get the team to go round to the shops on the main road and ask them for any footage which shows the gates to the park. Put out an appeal for witnesses and for any dashcam footage from drivers passing between six o'clock and ten o'clock. We'll review all the evidence at a briefing session in the next day or two. I'll be in late tomorrow — got something important to do.'

She looked at me quizzically.

'Ring me if you need to,' I said, feeling guilty, because she had put in a lot of hours too. *Must give her some time off when this case is wrapped up*, I thought.

'How's Lisa?' I asked Tim Lafferty on the phone later that day, as I drove west out of the city. It was early afternoon and I had finally caught up on some sleep.

'Just a scare, Rohan. Thought the baby might be premature. The contractions seemed to start. Doctor said it was Braxton Hicks — a false alarm, thank goodness. Lisa is under observation and I'm still at the hospital with her.'

'I'm sure it'll all be fine, Tim. Please give Lisa my best.'

'Thanks, Rohan. You're a good mate.'

I said I'd catch up with him soon and we said goodbye.

I glanced at the cage next to me on the passenger seat. 'Big day today, Fernando. It could change your life forever.' *And mine*, I thought.

His big, doleful eyes stared at me. He hadn't travelled in his cage for a while and he was probably confused. He couldn't see through the windows or windscreen and he instead gazed down into the passenger footwell. The cage bumped as I drove through a pothole.

'Sorry,' I said.

Half an hour later I turned onto a quiet country road, and entered a car park. The gravel rumbled under the tyres and some of it hit the underside of the car. I parked and took out Fernando's cage. The ear-splitting cacophony of hundreds of tropical birds, large and small, assaulted my ears as I walked into the main reception area of the Tropical Birds' Kingdom. As I was about to ring the bell, a door opened and a young woman wearing a cream fleece, blue jeans and a pair of wellington boots walked towards me, her hand outstretched.

'You must be Mr Sharma,' she said. 'I'm Bella. Lovely to meet you.' She looked at the cage. 'And this must be Fernando.'

I had rung the Kingdom earlier and explained my worries about Fernando and his excitement at seeing the other parrots on the television. They had suggested bringing Fernando in to have a look around.

Bella opened the cage door and stroked Fernando's head. He nuzzled his head against her hand.

'I see he likes you.'

'Shall we go in?' she suggested. Fernando hopped onto her shoulder. 'He's keen, isn't he?' Bella said with a smile.

We walked along the paths and through wooded areas.

'We have many varieties of tropical birds here, especially from the Amazon and from the rainforests of Central Africa,' Bella explained. 'We've got hornbills, macaws, parakeets, cockatoos, hoopoes, to name but a few. We also have nineteen African grey parrots. Most of the birds are fairly tame and they are free to roam freely. As you can see, visitors feed them nuts and seeds and the birds are happy.'

'How many African grey females have you got?'

'Of the nineteen, seven are female. Almost all were hatched in this country from eggs and then sold by pet shops. Some people like the idea of owning an exotic bird, but then soon get fed up with reality of having a noisy, messy bird in the house. They were either given to the RSPB or brought to us directly. We're anxious to broaden our gene pool so Fernando could be a great addition as he was born in the wild.' Fernando pulled her earlobe with his beak. She gently pushed him away. He nuzzled her neck. 'Lot of in-breeding in this country,' she said.

We walked on for a few minutes, past visitors feeding birds sitting on wooden poles along the path, mobile phone cameras doing overtime, people laughing, birds fluttering onto heads and outstretched arms.

'And here we are. Fernando will be really happy here with his new friends. And he will have plenty of girlfriends to choose from.'

Fernando gazed at the large enclosure which held at least a dozen African grey parrots. A few held on to the wire netting with their long claws, crunching the shells of groundnuts which the couple in front of us had given to them. Then there was silence as the parrots stared at Fernando.

'I think,' said Bella, 'he — and they — will need a period of acclimatisation. We'll introduce him gradually, so they can get to know each other. Why don't we go in? He'll be fine with both of us here.'

We entered the large enclosure. Seed trays hung down from wooden branches. Bird droppings and grass littered the floor. The African greys stopped munching their nuts and stared at us.

Fernando shot from Bella's shoulder and perched next to one of the parrots on a branch. He rubbed his body against her. Then he mounted her, his beak grabbing the gossamer feathers on her head.

Bella laughed. 'Well, he didn't waste any time, did he? No need for introductions there.'

'Fernando!' I said with a smile. 'You naughty boy.'

'Ah well, he's already found the one female in heat, so to speak. Don't think we'll have a problem expanding our gene pool with him here.'

I looked away, emotion suddenly overcoming me.

'I think everything'll be fine with Fernando, Mr Sharma,' Bella said sympathetically. 'But it's always hard making these decisions. Take as much time as you need. I do think he will be very happy here, though.'

'Thanks, Bella. I've been with him practically all my life.' I looked up. Fernando was now busy preening himself. He already looked happier. 'I want to do what's best for him. I work so much and I know he's lonely. I'll leave him here overnight, if that's okay, to see how he gets on?'

'Yes, of course. We'll keep you updated and you can visit him any time.'

She smiled and waved as I drove away. Fernando's empty cage sat on the seat next to me. My heart ached but it was cruel of me to keep him.

That evening, my front room was unusually quiet as I sipped Pinot Grigio and listened to Joni Mitchell, a lump in my throat. I tried to pull myself together when my mobile screen lit up and I saw Angie's name appear on it. I cleared my throat and answered.

'Sir, I think we've identified not one, but potentially two witnesses in the park,' she told me. 'The CCTV cameras picked up two cars and a white van. The white van had cloned number plates and we think it might have been used to transport the victim to the park. The other two cars, one a family saloon, the other an estate, we identified using the usual databases and we have the details of the owners. We have asked both to come into the station. Can you be there for nine o'clock tomorrow, please?'

'Yes, of course. Good work, Angie. Now get some rest. I'll see you tomorrow.'

CHAPTER 20

I hadn't heard from Bella and assumed Fernando was having the time of his life with his new harem. I had put off ringing her for an update, because I knew it would make me want to rush over there and I really had to let him go for his sake. He had looked so happy surrounded by others of his kind. I tried to push him out of my mind as I got ready for work and I was at my desk at police HQ by seven o'clock. I finished my report for Superintendent Breedon and had just sent it over to him when he walked into the room.

'Ah, good morning, Rohan. I see you're already hard at work.'

'I'm keen to learn from the example set by my superiors, Sir.'

His deep blue eyes bored into mine, trying to work out if I was being sarcastic or not. He decided not to say anything, so I briefed him on the latest developments.

'Thanks,' he said when I'd finished. 'We're briefing the Indian government and Kumar's family through the Downing Street channels, but there's pressure on the Chief Constable to solve the case quickly.'

'It takes as long as it takes, Sir. What d'you want me to do?'

Superintendent Breedon's moustache twitched. He cleared his throat. 'Just keep me posted,' he said, and walked out.

I desperately wanted a cup of tea but Angie had an update for me.

'We have two independent witnesses to interview about the body we found in the park,' she said, as we walked briskly to the interview room. 'I don't think they know each other. One's an Asian woman in her thirties, a nurse at the private hospital near the park, and the other's a Caucasian man who walks his dog in the park. We have the woman first.'

The informal interviews were taking place in the pink room, its soothing pastel shades, comfortable settees and vases full of bright flowers helping to make witnesses feel at ease. Angie and I walked in. The woman on the settee looked nervous. She made to stand up, but I gestured for her to remain sitting. I introduced myself, shook her hand, and asked if she wanted anything to drink. She declined.

'So, Mrs Bharti Gohil,' I began, sitting down and checking the notes Angie had placed in front of me. 'Thank you for coming in. Please understand, you're not a suspect but you might hold some important information about a serious crime. You were in the vicinity of the leisure park two nights ago?'

She nodded, her brown eyes flashing nervously from me to Angie. She fiddled with a rose-gold chain around her neck. 'How did you know I was there, Inspector Sharma?'

'CCTV cameras nearby picked up the number plate on your car. Can you tell me what time you reached the park and what you did when you got there?'

'I parked the car at about seven fifteen and went for a walk along the path in the park.'

'Do you usually walk in the park in the dark by yourself, Mrs Gohil?'

'There are plenty of lampposts along the path. My night shift was due to start at ten and my husband and I had had a row and the children were crying. I needed some fresh air.'

'I see. Did you notice any other vehicles in the car park when you got there?'

She paused. 'Yes, another car arrived not long after I did — a man and his dog. I don't think he saw me.'

'Did you see a white van, Mrs Gohil?'

She shook her head. 'No, I'm sorry, I didn't.'

'And how long do you think you were in the park?'

'Probably about twenty minutes. I'm not sure.'

I held her gaze. 'Is there anything else you can tell us, Mrs Gohil? Did you see anything unusual? Did you hear anything?'

She shook her head.

'Okay, thank you for coming in. An officer will take a full statement from you. Sergeant Deacon will accompany you.'

They left the room and I got some tea from the canteen. After a few minutes Angie walked back in with the second witness, David Newton. He was a tall man, who looked to be in his early forties. He explained that he arrived in the car park at about seven-twenty, got his dog out of the back of the estate, and let him run around a bit. He said he didn't see anyone, but he did remember another car parked nearby. There was nobody in it and he didn't give it much thought.

'Did you see a white van?'

'No, Inspector.' He rubbed his shaved head.

'What do you do for a living, Mr Newton?' asked Angie.

'I work at the big supermarket down the road from the park. I'm the manager of the fresh foods department. I do a lot of shift work there. But the other day was my day off.'

'Did you see or hear anything that could help us with our enquiries, Mr Newton?' I asked.

'No, sorry. I didn't really see anything.'

I explained that another officer would take a statement from him and he left.

A few moments later, Angie came back and sat down opposite me. 'They're both lying, Sir. The timing on the CCTV images shows that both of them arrived when they said they did, but both cars were in the car park for longer. Mrs Gohil's saloon was seen leaving at nineteen minutes past eight and Mr Newton's estate left at eight thirty-five.'

'Lovers' tryst?'

'Maybe, Sir.'

'Okay, Angie. Let's bring them back, but together this time.'

A few minutes later, both witnesses were sat next to each other on the settee opposite Angie and me. Bharti Gohil fiddled with her wedding ring, David Newton scratched his left arm.

'Okay, can you please tell us — truthfully this time — what you were both doing the night before yesterday please? And no lies. Because we know when both your cars arrived in the car park and when they left.'

'Please, Inspector Sharma, you won't tell my husband, will you?' Bharti pleaded. 'He doesn't even know I'm here. He thinks I am starting a morning shift.'

David Newton put his hand on her arm tenderly. 'Leave this to me, love,' he said.

He explained that they had agreed to meet at the park. Bharti had already parked and joined him in his estate when he arrived. They had been intimate together and the windows had steamed up. As they were about to get dressed and raise the seats again, they heard the sound of an engine.

'I rubbed the steam from one of the windows and looked out,' David continued. 'A white van parked up and two people got out. A man and a woman, I think. The man had a pistol in his hand. The woman had a long metal pole in hers. They forced a second man in the back of the van to get out. His hands were tied. They led him into the park. I told Bharti to keep quiet, while I followed at a distance.

'When they got to the roundabout in the children's playground, they told the man to lie down on it, face down. He was crying, telling them not to do anything. The woman then put the metal pole at an angle under the wheel. I thought that was strange.'

'Can you describe them?' asked Angie.

'The man looked to be white, with short hair, could have been blond. The woman wore dark jeans, a dark coat and her face was covered. You know the gear Muslim women wear? Looked a bit like that.'

'A *hijab*, you mean?' asked Angie.

'Yes ... and then the man lying on the wheel — I couldn't see what he looked like — he told the other man not to do anything. But then...'

'Then?' I asked.

'The woman took the pistol and shot him in the back of the head. They untied the dead man, turned him over and left. I was really scared. As soon as they left I ran back to the car and we both got out right quick.'

'David didn't tell me anything at the time,' said Mrs Gohil, holding his hand. 'He didn't want to scare me. I didn't know much about what had happened in the park until I heard about it on the news the next day. Please don't tell my husband about us, will you? Oh, God ... what've we done, David?'

I looked into her wide eyes. I tried not to think of what Faye had done, meeting Pierre behind my back while I spent every hour working. It had resulted in the end of our marriage, the end of our family unit. But then, how much had I contributed to the destruction of our marriage? I tried not to think about what had driven Faye to do what she did.

'I'm married too. My wife would be devastated if she found out,' said David Newton. He clutched Bharti Gohil's hand.

I tried not to dwell on my conflicting emotions. I thanked them for speaking to us. I asked Angie to take a full statement from them both and left.

CHAPTER 21

I arrived early at police HQ the next morning, grabbed a cup of tea and strode into the incident room where I had arranged a briefing on the case. It was empty apart from a familiar figure sitting at the end of the long conference table, her laptop switched on.

'Nasreen! How lovely to see you. I wasn't expecting to see anyone here yet.'

'Good morning, Rohan. Good to see you, too.'

I took a seat opposite her. 'It really is good to have you back,' I said. 'How are you settling into your new place?'

'Would be doing even better if I wasn't getting called out late at night to look at dead bodies,' she said with a smile. 'Plays havoc with unpacking. Still, can't be helped. The victims don't go out of their way to ruin my private life.'

'No, but they could be more considerate,' I replied.

She grinned. 'And what about you, Rohan? How's your new girlfriend?'

'Anita? We get on really well,' I replied. 'That is when we manage to meet. But I haven't seen her for a little while. And I'm trying my best to do what I can for my children while working all hours at this job. I ended up giving up Fernando.' I explained about the tropical bird sanctuary. 'How about you, Nasreen? How are you doing?'

Her eyes lingered on mine for a long time before she looked away. 'I prefer to work with the dead,' she said, her voice trembling. 'At least they can't hurt you or break your heart.'

The only sound in the room was the whir from her laptop fan.

'No, they don't break your heart,' I eventually replied. 'But the dead always take a part of your heart with them.'

Nasreen turned the diamond ring on her finger, was about to say something when the door opened and the others walked in.

I invited them all to sit down as I stood up and took the chair at the head of the table, the digital smartboard behind me.

When they were all paying attention, like a class waiting for the lesson to start, I said, 'Thanks for attending this briefing session. I thought it was time we compared notes, reviewed the evidence, and decided what we need to do next. We know that Sunil Kumar was poisoned with ricin via a pellet made from platinum and iridium. The pellet was fired into his right shoulder by a man in a turban, whose real identity we are still trying to establish. Mr Kumar's final words to me were that ISIS killed him. Or so it sounded to me at the time.

'Ali, as our informer called him, was already known to our secret services as a Muslim extremist and drug dealer. He had undergone plastic surgery on his face recently, suggesting he was trying to prevent us from identifying him. He himself was killed by two men, one of whom was white with short blond hair. He was shot in the back by a pistol, but the shot didn't kill him — he was asphyxiated. The blond-haired man had a tattoo with the letters *A* and *H* in a circle on his arm. This symbol was also found sprayed on the wall near where *The Turbanator* met his end. MI5 believe it refers to Abdul Hussain's extremist group. They've been active in other parts of the world and have left the same symbol there.'

'Sorry, Sir, do you mind if I interject?' asked Ben Carter. I nodded for him to continue. '*The Turbanator* was shot by a thirty-eight calibre bullet from a Smith and Wesson pistol.

There was no other forensic evidence of significance in the area. We haven't tracked down the pistol yet.'

'Thank you, Ben,' I said, before continuing. 'We don't yet know the link between Mr Kumar and *The Turbanator*, although I've been given information that suggests Mr Kumar was involved in some of the same shady dealings, including trafficking or financing illegal drugs. What we do know is that something strange happened during his journey to the UK. CCTV footage shows that a suitcase was thrown into the luggage hold at Prague Airport where the plane had a made a refuelling stop. The same suitcase was then taken off the plane here in the UK by the man with the short blond hair and was taken through a gap in the fence. We don't know yet what was in the suitcase.'

'No, we don't,' said Tim, bags under tired brown eyes, 'but it could well be drugs, given what we now know about Sunil Kumar. Drugs fund extremist activities. There might have been some double-dealing, which led to Mr Kumar's death, but we don't know for certain. I spoke to Cynthia from MI5 yesterday evening and she said they didn't have anything new to add at this stage. But we do know there's plenty of chatter — both online and through our informers — that something's being planned for Leicester.'

'Thanks, Tim. The chatter about Leicester is concerning, so we'll keep a close eye on that. Then there's the guy with the blond hair and tattoo — who is he? A convert to the cause? And we have the case of the Kumars' missing holdall. The chauffeur drove off with it after dropping the Kumars at the Regency Hotel. Was that an innocent mistake? Mrs Kumar said the holdall was returned several hours later and nothing was missing.'

'Perhaps we're reading too much into it, Sir,' said Angie. 'The chauffeur and his brother are not on our radar for anything. Just a couple of hard-working guys running a family business.'

'You may well be right, Angie,' I replied. 'But I don't like loose ends. At least we can say that Cyril Braganza's death was straightforward. It was very sad, but it seems he took his own life after the shame of being arrested.'

A few heads in the room nodded.

'And now,' continued Angie, 'we have the unidentified Middle Eastern man found dead on the roundabout in the park. Appeals for information have been put out, but we've had no promising leads so far. Nobody has reported anyone fitting his description as missing.'

'He was shot in the back of the head — again with a thirty-eight calibre bullet,' said Ben. 'Ballistics tests reveal it came from the same gun as the one used on *The Turbanator* — a Smith and Wesson pistol. The barrel marks on the bullet are the same.'

'And,' said Nasreen, 'that was the cause of death in this case.'

'So we know the deaths are linked, and witnesses place the blond man at both crime scenes,' I said, 'but we don't yet know who he is. David Newton — the witness at the park — claims that our victim was shot by a woman wearing a *hijab*. But no symbol was spray-painted near the body. The two killers travelled to the park in a white van. Needless to say, they used cloned number plates.'

'What's the motive?' asked Tim, his frustration evident. 'There's no pattern to the killings.'

The room was silent.

'Jamie,' I said. 'Let's take a look at the drone footage from the park.'

Jamie clicked his mouse a couple of times and the monitor behind me flickered. I moved my chair out of the way and we all looked at the screen. The camera on the drone hovered over the body as forensic officers in white suits moved around the ship's wheel.

'Pause it there, will you please, Jamie?' I said. 'I think I've noticed something.' The image on the screen showed the victim on the roundabout, his arms and legs stretched out. 'Jamie, can you rotate the image for me?'

He did so. There were gasps as the others saw it too.

The body was now perpendicular to us. The long metal rod, bent at a right angle at one end, rested just below the waist and ran all the way under the left shoulder. There was no mistaking it. The body had been positioned in such a way that it looked like the symbol in the disused warehouse when we found the body of *The Turbanator*.

The crimes had to be linked. But what was the message and who the hell were the killers? Just as I was grappling with these thoughts, Angie's mobile vibrated.

'Sorry, Sir. Got to take this. Will be back in a moment.' She went out.

The rest of us discussed things further but weren't getting very far. Angie walked back into the room a few minutes later. She had a big smile on her face.

'I think we may have a breakthrough, Sir. The Missing Persons Unit have a possible name for our park victim. Jihan Mirza. Went missing a week ago in London.'

'Thanks, Angie. Good work.'

I wound up the meeting. I asked Tim as he was leaving if everything was okay with Lisa and the baby. He nodded and said he'd catch up with me before too long. Angie followed him out, and Ben and Jamie left with her.

I smiled at Nasreen as she packed up. 'It's good to see you happy again, Nasreen.'

Her bottom lip trembled. 'I know, Rohan. Thank you for caring. It's good to be back.'

I met Angie in the mortuary foyer later that morning.

'So, we think our victim's from London, do we?' I asked.

'Yes, Sir. Jihan Mirza went missing a week ago from his flat in central London. His wife Shahnaz and family members have been frantic with worry. They put out appeals on social media but only reported him missing three days ago. The MPU in the Met alerted the wife that a man matching her husband's description had been found deceased in Leicester. An officer is accompanying them and they'll be here soon.'

'Who's they?'

'Shahnaz Mirza, their daughter Ettie who's twenty-one, and the sister of the deceased, Gulzaar.'

We sat down to wait for the family to arrive. Eventually, one of the swing doors was pushed open.

Three women came rushing towards Angie and me. A female DC from the Met followed at a more leisurely pace. We introduced ourselves and, after offering them a drink, I said, 'Mrs Mirza, we don't yet know for certain if the man we found is your husband. I'm hoping it isn't. But we obviously need to know one way or another.'

Shahnaz Mirza nodded. Her face was full of fear. Her daughter Ettie hugged her, while Gulzaar's hands trembled, her honey-coloured eyes filled with tears. I explained that Sergeant Deacon would accompany them to the viewing area. As the only male present, I decided to remain outside.

Angie opened the mortuary door. Each of the women passed through. I waited.

A few minutes later, the inevitable wail pierced my heart. I sighed and closed my eyes.

The women finally emerged, comforting each other, tears streaming down their cheeks. I gestured for them to sit down while Angie fetched some drinks. After a little while we moved to an adjoining room where I could conduct an informal interview.

'I know this must be incredibly difficult for you, Mrs Mirza,' I began when they were all settled. 'But we need to find out who did this to your husband. We need to ask you some questions to help with that. Would you like to wait for a while? Or are you okay to do this now?'

She stared at me. Her hands clutched at a tissue. She nodded.

'What can you tell us about your husband?' I asked. 'His life. His work. Friends, that sort of thing.'

Shahnaz stared at the tissue in her hands and started twisting and turning it.

'Inspector Sharma,' said Gulzaar, 'my brother Jihan was forty-six years old. We came to London with our father after escaping from Iran when Jihan was eleven. Our father worked for the Shah before the ayatollahs toppled him in 1979, so his cards were always marked. He was constantly harassed by the police, in and out of jail, beaten, accused of being a traitor, accused of being a non-believer. Eventually he managed to escape with us, first to Azerbaijan, then to Lithuania, before we finally arrived in London. He borrowed money from other Iranian people here, set up an import and export business — carpets, perfume, furniture — and started making money. From there he moved into property development, which is where he made his money.'

'What about your brother, Jihan? How did he find the move to the UK?' asked Angie.

'We had a happy childhood. We were enrolled in state schools at first but then transferred to private schools when our father had more money. Jihan was always happy at school; he played football and rugby to a high standard, and then did a joint degree in mechanical engineering and chemistry at Imperial College, London. He did plenty of post-graduate research afterwards and got a position as a lecturer there. He was very clever. Everybody said he should have applied to Oxford or Cambridge but he wanted to stay in London. He had plenty of friends and a good social life. Then he met Shahnaz through family contacts. They got married when Jihan was twenty-two and she was twenty-one. They've had such a happy life. And graced by the birth of a beautiful daughter... Who could have done this to us?' She started sobbing.

Ettie hugged her aunt. Shahnaz, wide-eyed, broken-hearted, stared straight ahead.

'Jihan was always researching and working,' Shahnaz eventually said. 'Both here and in universities in other parts of the world. Israel, Pakistan, Turkey, Syria. He was away for many weeks sometimes. Especially in our summer when the universities were closed for a long time.'

'Who paid for all the travel? His other costs?' I decided not to say anything about the possible cost of their London residence.

Ettie spoke for the first time. 'My dad was highly thought of in his field, and companies abroad paid a lot for his services.'

'What exactly was his field?' I asked.

'Metal stress,' Ettie replied. 'How metal stress in oil pipelines and in aeroplanes and rockets could be improved.'

'Why was he in Leicester? Did he mention knowing anyone at the university here? Or did he work with any companies in the city?'

'He once did some work at Loughborough University,' said Shahnaz. 'But that was a long time ago. Maybe four or five years ago. There was no reason for him to be here, but he once said he was doing something *for* Leicester, not *in* Leicester. It didn't make sense to me so I didn't ask any further. Why would somebody want to kill him?' She started sobbing again.

'That's what we're going to find out, Mrs Mirza,' I said. 'Do the letters *A H* mean anything to you?'

Shahnaz stared at me for a long time and then she shook her head.

'Did your husband ever go back to Iran? Work? Family?'

'You've got to be kidding, Inspector,' replied Gulzaar. 'It's far too dangerous for exiles like us to return there.'

I expressed my condolences again and thanked them for their time. I didn't think there would be a delay in releasing the body by the coroner, because the cause of death was quite clear.

I asked Angie to set up appropriate support arrangements for the family, to liaise with the Met and to speak to all known work colleagues of the victim.

Later that evening, I chilled a bottle of Veuve Clicquot, and frosted a couple of long-stemmed champagne flutes in the freezer. Then I spoke to Yasmin and Karan, asked them about school, about their day, what they might want for Christmas and they said they'd like to meet up with me so we could do something special — just the three of us. Karan said he had already started rehearsing in the school nativity play for Christmas and he was playing one of the wise men from the

East 'because of the colour of my skin' and because some of the boys said he was 'fat and rich'. I told him that was not the case and he shouldn't pay much attention to what the other children were saying. 'They're just jealous,' I said, knowing how feeble that sounded. I made a mental note to speak to Faye about it.

The front door clicked open as I ended the call. Anita breezed into the room, pulling a small travelling case behind her. 'God, parking round here's so difficult, Rohan.'

'And hello to you, too,' I said and smiled. 'I know, I'm sorry I couldn't save you a spot outside. There would've been a riot if I'd tried.'

We hugged and didn't let each other go.

After a while, I said, 'Why don't you freshen up, have a shower if you want to, and I'll order some food? Got the champagne ready. I want to make up for not seeing you on Sunday.'

Anita smiled, gave me a kiss and left the room.

When she came back down, she had changed into a pair of jeans and a flattering top. She sat down next to me on the settee and we raised our glasses.

'It's so lovely to see you,' I said.

'Ditto,' she said. 'But where's Fernando?'

I explained what had happened.

'You didn't get rid of him because of me, did you?' she asked, concerned. 'I know he was struggling with me being here, but you've had him forever.'

'No, it wasn't your fault,' I assured her. 'I realised that he didn't seem his old self. He was desperate for attention and now that I don't live with the kids, he doesn't get enough of it. He'll get plenty at the bird sanctuary.'

'Are you okay?' she asked, squeezing my arm.

'Not really,' I sighed, 'but much better now you're here.'

A couple of hours later, we were lying in bed, Anita's head resting on my shoulder. Her warm body was pressed against mine and her steady breathing suggested she had fallen asleep. I wondered whether she was dreaming. Strands of her hair tickled my neck and I shifted uneasily, trying to ignore it. I looked up at the ghostly outline of the two dodos on the Artexed ceiling in the faint glow from the streetlight outside. I thought of how long ago the birds had become extinct. Whether the last one knew it was the last in the world. If only a mate had survived, the species could have been revived. I thought of Fernando and wondered if he was fast asleep, similarly sated. Eventually, trying not to dwell on the fate of the dodos, I drifted off to sleep.

'Come on, Rohan, wakey, wakey,' said Anita. I opened my weary eyes as she passed me a cup of tea. I thanked her and slowly got out of bed. Over breakfast, we chatted and I went through the salient details of the case with her. I had no problem in her maintaining confidentiality and I knew she might think of things which I may have overlooked. I told her I wasn't sure if Mr Mirza was involved in the drugs trade or something else, given his Middle Eastern connections.

'Well, I can help find that out for you,' she said.

'What?'

'Our troops, especially the Royal Marines and sometimes the Parachute Regiment, are often involved in monitoring such activities. It gives them a good excuse to be near enemy territory, gathering intelligence about all sorts of things.'

'Anita, that's wonderful. It would be really helpful if you could find anything out. On the QT, of course. Nothing official.'

'Okay. I'll ring a couple of senior officers once I get dressed.'

I kissed her.

We had a quiet morning. Anita made a few phone calls, while I watched some cricket from Australia. I tried not to long for the gloriously sunny weather Down Under while the days were getting short in the northern hemisphere.

'All right, Sherlock,' Anita said, after ending the last call. 'I spoke to a couple of majors, one in the Marines and the other in the Paras. They've been monitoring a container ship recently which is supposed to be transporting heroin worth millions. The drugs usually come overland from Afghanistan to Iran and then to the Persian Gulf. Our secret services were also working with the two regiments tracking one particular lorry, but the bug planted in it went dead in Iran. The Iranian authorities might have discovered it. They're obviously involved in the trade because it brings them lucrative foreign currency, mainly American dollars.'

'Don't tell me,' I said. 'The bug went dead in Isfahan.'

'Yes,' she said. 'How did you know?'

I explained that Cynthia, the MI5 officer, had mentioned something similar a few days ago. 'This case gets knottier and knottier, Anita. How was Mr Mirza, an Iranian exile, involved? Given his scientific background, was he perhaps processing the opium? Could a lucrative shipment have made its way to Prague? The extra suitcase which was thrown into the luggage hold?'

Anita shrugged. 'You need a break. Let's go out and have a good time.'

And we did. It was lovely to do some normal things for a change. To go shopping. To laugh. To go to the cinema. To drink more champagne. To go to bed early. And not just to go to sleep.

All too soon, Anita had to leave for work. I was left in an empty house with an empty heart. It felt desolate without her and without Fernando.

CHAPTER 22

The next day, I had a briefing session with Tim and Angie. We agreed to dig into the background of the dead scientist and to review all the evidence we had so far, but after a few frustrating hours with no further discoveries, we called it a day.

The evening found me back at The Omar Khayyam. The restaurant was decorated with expensive Persian rugs and silver shisha pipes with long tubes to drag the smoke into your lungs. Those downstairs were for decorative purposes only but customers could use the shisha bar upstairs if they so wished — since tobacco was not used, it did not break the law. Being early in the evening and on a weekday, there were only two other customers. Mr Rahimi shook my hand and showed me to a candle-lit table away from the others, as I requested.

I washed my hands in a round steel bowl full of warm water and red rose petals. Mr Rahimi passed me a towel to dry my hands and handed me the menu.

'Thank you so much, Mr Rahimi. I'm meeting a friend.'

He smiled and waved his forefinger at me. 'Another pretty lady, Mr Rohan? I'm surprised you're not married again.'

'The same lady. I'm meeting her about work, Mr Rahimi. All to do with work.'

'That's what they all say,' he replied, and winked.

'But tell me something,' I said. 'The exiled Iranian community in this country is close-knit. Is that right?'

'Yes, it is close-knit. We all know each other. Also others elsewhere in Europe, America, Canada. Sometimes some of us get together in London for a meal, for a celebration. Many sons and daughters of the original exiles — people like me — have married each other and started their own families in different parts of the world. Why do you ask, Mr Rohan?'

'Have you heard of a Mr Jihan Mirza? A scientist? Worked in London at Imperial College? He came here after the Shah was deposed.'

'Jihan Mirza? No, I have not heard of him. He wasn't the man found dead in the park, was he? I heard about that on the news.'

I confirmed that he was.

'I can ask around some more,' said Mr Rahimi. 'See if anybody else has heard of him.'

'Thank you. Please let me know if you hear of anything.' I gave him my mobile number. 'We found out he had dual citizenship, British and Iranian, and that he was born in the town of Shiraz. That's in the south-west of the country, isn't it?'

Mr Rahimi nodded. 'Be careful, Mr Rohan. It is very unusual for the son of an exile to be granted an Iranian passport. The authorities in Iran wouldn't trust them... You may be dealing with forces you do not understand. You're like a cat, Mr Rohan. Always curious. I know it's your job, but a cat does not always have nine lives.'

The door opened. I looked up and Mr Rahimi turned around.

'Ah, your pretty friend is here.'

I waved to Meena Patel and beckoned her over. I thanked her for coming from Birmingham at relatively short notice. We both ordered soft drinks, and then ordered some food. She was curious about the developments in the case so far and was particularly interested in Jihan Mirza, but I was wary about giving too much away.

Eventually, she said, 'Look, Rohan, I don't know why you asked me to make the journey here on this dark and miserable evening. I thought you were going to tell me something new, but you're playing your cards close to your chest.' Her brown eyes shimmered in the flickering candlelight. Her foot brushed mine under the table. 'Okay,' she continued, 'why don't we agree to share information?'

'How do I know I can trust you? Is RAW still monitoring my phone?'

She shrugged. 'As I said before, that's way above my pay grade. I have no idea. Anyway, I saw you were using a different number when you rang me earlier today.'

I smiled. 'Can't be too careful, Meena.'

'Cards on the table?' she asked.

I nodded.

'I like you, Rohan, and I believe you want to solve this case as soon as possible. I know there's a lot of political pressure on you, both from the Indian government and from Downing Street. We can't do anything in this country, but we can help you. *I* can help you.'

The small red *tiki* on her forehead moved up and down.

'Go on,' I said.

'As you know, we're keeping an eye on ISI, the Pakistani secret service, both here and in other parts of the world. And you think that Sunil Kumar may have said ISIS or ISI to you as he lay dying. ISI have been involved in a number of terrorist activities against India. We think they're up to something again but we're not sure what. What complicates things is that a small number of ISI agents have gone rogue and they're doing their own thing. The Pakistani government and the rest of the military — who hold the real power — know there are rogue agents and are trying to track them down. They may not have them yet.'

'What has this got to do with me, Meena?'

Her bright brown eyes smiled at me across the table. 'What this has to do with you,' she said, 'is the drugs trade. The agents in ISI are using drugs from Afghanistan — the heroin poppy — to finance their activities and those of some extremist groups. The usual roads of shipping the drugs from Afghanistan to Pakistan are not being used at the moment to show the West that Pakistan is helping in the anti-drugs trade. But what's happening is that new channels have opened up into Iran and some corrupt officials in the Iranian government are taking a cut. It's developing into a lucrative trade worth millions. The trade, sadly, also involves human trafficking. You can guess what for.'

Our main course of lamb with vine leaves for me, and chicken with olives for Meena arrived, accompanied with rice cooked with sultanas and saffron. As we started eating, I updated Meena on the progress of the case but left out a few critical details. I still didn't trust her, despite the occasional brush of my leg under the table and the long, lingering looks. Maybe I was being too suspicious. I asked, 'Do you think the scientist Jihan Mirza was involved in the processing of raw opium into heroin for the ISI? Or even for the Iranians?'

'Possibly yes, to both. There are plenty of good laboratories, both in Pakistan and Iran. They would speed up the process of refining the opium and produce pure heroin. High grade. This could then be mixed with other things to increase profit margins. Mr Mirza would be well-placed to do something like this because of his knowledge of chemistry.'

I told her about Jihan Mirza's dual nationality.

'That's very unusual for the son of an exile,' she said, echoing Mr Rahimi sentiments. 'He could be a double agent. Planted — or turned — by the Iranian government.

'So, if Jihan Mirza was involved in making pure heroin,' I said, 'what was Sunil Kumar's role?'

'We're working on that. But first a history lesson. As you know, India, Pakistan and Bangladesh were all one country until the British partitioned them in 1947. Sunil Kumar's ancestors were originally Muslims from Lahore. His great-grandfather was a budding actor who knew the Pakistan film industry was heading nowhere compared to Bollywood, so he changed his name from Akmal Durrani to Prem Kumar, a solid Hindu name. Over time he achieved great success in the 1940s and 1950s and the Muslim identity was soon gone. His son followed in his father's footsteps, as did the rest. Now the family is as Hindu as you can get. The cameras are always there when they go to pray in temples, celebrate Diwali or when they welcome Hindu holy men into their houses.'

'That's interesting. My mother will be very upset,' I said with a smile.

'Many Hindus would be if they found out the truth,' Meena said. 'Anyway, thanks for the meal, Rohan. I'm off.'

'What? Why're you leaving?'

'I've given you a lot but you're not giving much in return.'

CHAPTER 23

I woke after a restless night, still thinking about my meeting with Meena Patel. I really needed to keep her onside so she would tell me of any new developments about Sunil Kumar. I rang her phone a few times and eventually, she picked up.

'Look, Rohan, I left because I can't trust you.'

'What? Look who's talking.'

'I was being honest with you last night, but I could tell you were holding back. I told you some time ago I try to be honourable in a dishonourable business.'

'Try to?'

'Well, it's not always easy, but yes, I try to. You've entered a world which I don't think you fully understand. And which is very dangerous.'

'Okay, Meena. I'm sorry. But it's freaking me out that your lot are monitoring my phone. God knows what else they're doing. Please get them to stop. I'm a British police officer and what they're doing is illegal.'

'I don't think that's going to help you. But I'll see what I can do. By the way, I think the Pakistani secret service is the least of your worries. We may be working on the same side.'

'Can we meet again, please? I'll come to Birmingham this time.'

She agreed and I said I'd get back to her when I had time to drive over.

As I ended the call, my phone rang. It was Bella from the Tropical Birds' Kingdom.

'I'm sorry to ring so early in the morning, Mr Sharma, but you need to come here quickly.'

'Why?' I asked, concerned. 'Is Fernando spreading his genes a bit too freely?'

When she told me he had been attacked, I rushed to the car and drove straight there. Bella was waiting for me in front of the large enclosure with the African grey parrots. I searched for Fernando but couldn't see him among the others.

Bella smiled nervously at me. 'He's not there, Mr Sharma. I've had to put him in a cage by himself. Please come with me.'

She led me through a storehouse filled with sacks of grain, walnuts and groundnuts, and we eventually arrived in a small room at the back. A row of wire cages housed various birds, some being fed liquid through a plastic syringe by a ranger. It smelled of sawdust and bird droppings. Fernando sat on the perch in the middle of a small cage. He looked up at me and then looked down again.

'Oh, Fernando...' I said, taking him out of the cage and stroking him gently. He looked at me and blinked, his eyes moist. He had lost weight and some of the grey and white feathers around his neck and head were missing. Dried blood had congealed around the back of his neck.

'I'm really sorry, Mr Sharma. Everything seemed fine at first but then one of the male parrots started attacking him. The others joined in and wouldn't let him near the females. We removed the other males from the cage at times, but then some of the females started attacking him, too. They probably regarded Fernando as a threat to their territory. Because he's domesticated and hasn't had any experience of living with other African greys, he doesn't know how to defend himself. In the end, Fernando gave up, wouldn't eat and had difficulty sleeping. I'm not sure we can do anything more, Mr Sharma. I'm sorry.'

'That's all right, Bella. I'm sure you and your colleagues did your best. It seemed a good idea to bring Fernando here, but clearly I got that wrong.'

'I'm sure he'll settle down once he's back home,' she said. 'In surroundings where he's more comfortable. His weight will pick up again, the feathers will grow before too long. Please contact me for advice if you need to.'

I thanked her, put Fernando's cage on the passenger seat and drove back towards Leicester. 'I'm so sorry, Fernando. I thought you'd be happier there.' I felt guilty. He hadn't spoken since I'd arrived, and now just stared into the passenger footwell.

It was late morning as I turned into my street. I didn't want to leave Fernando by himself and asked the usual neighbours, Mr and Mrs Chand, to look after him for a few hours. They were happy to do so.

I called Meena and told her I would take the train into Birmingham. She said she would text me a meeting place.

Sometime later, my train pulled into New Street Station. I walked past the Town Hall and a few minutes later into a wine bar on Broad Street.

Meena sat at a table in a quiet corner, away from the handful of other customers in the bar. I waved to her, sat down opposite, and asked her what she wanted to eat and drink.

'I see you're in your business suit,' I said, once we had our drinks and had placed our order.

She smiled.

'Business is business,' she said. She leaned forward and formed a steeple with her fingers. 'I see you believe in the same.'

'I'm sorry about yesterday. But it wasn't all my fault,' I said.

She sipped her fruit mocktail from the tall glass.

'Let bygones be bygones,' she said. 'Let's try again, shall we.' Her big, brown eyes rested on mine. 'Do you remember me telling you Sunil Kumar's great-grandfather came from an area in what is now Pakistan? Well, our Mr Kumar found some old photographs of the family in Lahore, all wearing traditional Muslim clothes. He became interested in discovering more about his roots. After learning of the atrocities committed by Indian troops in Kashmir, the killing of some Muslims in other parts of India who were accused by the Hindu nationalists of selling beef and leather, and the destruction of mosques and replacement with Hindu temples and so on, he decided he didn't want to live a lie anymore. And wanted to do something about it.'

'How do you know this?'

She didn't reply, just smiled.

'But you work for the Indian government?'

'That doesn't mean I agree with everything they do. But I remain quiet. See, I'm being honourable with you.'

I returned her smile.

'Anyway, my government is becoming more repressive towards Muslims. In certain parts, like Assam, which borders Myanmar and Bangladesh, they're de-registering Muslim families from the population census. Without such recognition, the Muslim people have become refugees in their own country, somewhere they've lived for hundreds of years.'

'So, Sunil Kumar was doing his bit,' I said. 'Buying and selling drugs. Making millions. All the while maintaining a façade — going to the temple to pray, celebrating Diwali.'

'He had access to prominent politicians and high-level police and armed forces personnel. As you know, in India, a Bollywood star is next to a god. He may have been pumping them for information, or offering them kickbacks. He may well

155

have been turned by the rogue ISI agents in Pakistan. He would've been a great asset for them. Widely travelled, invited to parties at foreign Indian embassies, meeting foreign politicians, and so on. We think the money from the drugs trade was being used to finance insurrection movements like ISIS, Al-Shabab and Boko Haram.'

'So why kill him if he was such a valuable asset to them?'

'Perhaps he double-crossed them on a drugs deal. He might've planned a few deals without letting ISI know what was happening. After all, he needed them for a safe passage for the drugs or raw opium in Pakistan and then into Iran next door. But if nobody knew, it wouldn't matter. And he'd have pocketed millions. Perhaps they found out. Killed him. Easier to do it here in the UK. In India, he lived in a heavily fortified house with many security guards. It would've been difficult to get to him. And if it came out that a Muslim from Pakistan, or even from India, had killed him, ironically it would have led to the killing of more Muslims by Hindus.'

'This is mostly conjecture though, isn't it?' I asked.

Meena looked out of the large window before turning back to me. 'Some of it is based on evidence. Some of it is conjecture at this stage. But what I told you fits all the known facts.'

'What about the man who killed him?'

'We knew he was a Muslim extremist from our monitoring of his close activities with ISI. We kept a watch on his family, used informers, monitored bank accounts, his travels, so on. But we had no idea he was here. Probably because of the plastic surgery he had undergone recently. His real name was Umar Rizwan. He worked a lot with ISI in various parts of the world. We're trying to locate Abdul Hussain and Mohammed Jahangir. But we've no idea where they are.'

'So Umar Rizwan and Sunil Kumar were both working with ISI, and probably helping them to traffic drugs.'

'What's interesting,' Meena continued, 'is that Kumar's plane was due to refuel at Zurich in the original flight plan submitted at Mumbai Airport. This was changed to Prague at the very last minute. We don't know why. My RAW colleagues spoke to the pilot in India and he said he was following Sunil Kumar's instructions. He didn't question these and it made no difference to him where the plane was refuelled. The two cities are not that far apart.'

'What about the scientist, Jihan Mirza? What's his role in all of this?'

'We've no idea. Couldn't get a positive ID on him. And that, my dear Rohan, is that. For the time being.'

Meena said she had to get back to the office and I ordered a taxi for her. I made my way back to New Street Station. I sat in the cavernous concourse waiting for the next train to Leicester. I looked up and thought of a long-lost love I used to meet at a café upstairs for lunch. I wondered what had become of her.

My phone rang. I put my earbuds in to filter out the noise.

'Mr Rohan, Mr Rahimi here. Just to say, I make some enquiries about Mr Mirza. Two people in London have heard of him but know very little about him. He kept himself to himself. Didn't attend any gatherings of exiles. Sounds suspicious, no?'

'Maybe. Thank you, Mr Rahimi. Please let me know if you hear anything else.'

As I sat down on my upgraded first-class seat, which I paid for myself to get a bit of comfort and privacy, Angie rang.

'Been looking at Jihan Mirza's bank accounts, Sir. Had to pull all the stops out to get them. Anyway, Mr Mirza's salary as an academic was definitely not enough to pay for the central

London flat, or his jet set lifestyle. If universities or other organisations paid for him, there's no record of this in the transactions.'

'Maybe they sent him the air tickets directly?'

'Could've done, but why go to all that trouble? Why not just pay him and let him make all the arrangements? There's no record of him claiming back significant sums of money on his expenses. It had to come from somewhere else.'

'Thanks, Angie. Please keep digging. Speak soon. I've got another call waiting. Oh, and I'm not available tomorrow. Please don't contact me unless it's a matter of life or death.'

She said she understood and cut the call.

'Rohan,' said Tim Lafferty when I answered. 'I've been speaking to Cynthia and her view is that Mirza was probably a double agent. MI6 confirm he had at least one bank account in Switzerland but they couldn't hack into it so they don't know what kind of transactions occurred. No need for a simple academic to have a Swiss bank account, is there? By the way, we're picking up a lot of intel that whatever is being planned in Leicester is going to happen soon. We still don't know what exactly it is, but we're working on it.'

I thanked him and cut the connection. I rang my neighbours to check on Fernando and they said he was quiet but okay. That he had munched a few pieces of apple and had eaten some pumpkin seeds.

I reclined my comfortable seat, closed my eyes and listened to Leonard Cohen through the earbuds. I nodded off and woke up with the conductor's announcement when the train stopped at Leicester station.

I picked up Fernando from my neighbours in the early evening and took him home. He sat on the edge of the settee while I

158

diced plenty of pineapple and apple, and put out copious amounts of pumpkin and sunflower seeds.

'Come on, Fernando. Please eat something,' I coaxed, as I pushed the two trays towards him. 'Please?'

His scrawny neck with the red sores twisted sideways. He looked at me with big, round eyes.

'Please, Fernando, you're back home now. We'll soon have you better. Mr and Mrs Chand said you were eating at their house. Why won't you eat here?'

He flew to his cage, sat on his perch, folded his wings and closed his eyes.

It broke my heart.

I tried to eat some leftovers from the fridge, thinking he might follow my example, but he kept his eyes closed. I made a few phone calls. Spoke to my parents, spoke to Yasmin and Karan, and had a quick word with my ex-wife, Faye, about my concerns about Karan. She said she would speak to the school, but I told her not to do that yet, as it could just make things worse for him.

As I went up to bed later, I wondered if Fernando would be better staying in the bedroom with me. But he was sleepy and I decided to leave him downstairs. If he wanted me for anything, he knew where to find me.

CHAPTER 24

I woke up early the next day and cleaned out Fernando's cage as he perched on the window ledge. He had eaten some fruit and there were a few groundnut shells on the newspaper lining his cage.

'Good boy, Fernando.'

He carried on watching the world outside, while I sat down to eat my muesli in front of the news. I stopped munching. A still photograph of my face had suddenly filled the television screen. I turned the volume up.

'The Indian government has asked the British government to order an external review into the death of the Bollywood icon, Mr Sunil Kumar, who was murdered in Leicestershire. A spokesman for the Indian government said progress in arresting the killer or killers is slow and another police force should review how the case has been handled by the senior investigating officer, Detective Inspector Rohan Sharma, and his team. We approached Inspector Sharma for an interview but he was unavailable. His immediate superior, Superintendent Breedon, stated he and the senior leadership had full confidence in the way the case has been handled and they saw no need for an external review. For now… And onto other news…'

I grabbed my phone.

Superintendent Breedon picked up on the third ring.

'What the hell's going on, Sir? I was never asked for an interview by the television station.'

'Good morning, Rohan. They did request one, but we decided you were too busy to answer their questions. I thought I'd speak to them to keep them at bay.'

'And what's this "for now" business? Do you want to have an external review?'

'Look, Rohan, the heat's on from Downing Street and the Home Office. They want this case wrapped up.'

'So do I. We're all doing our best to solve it. We can't just pin this on an innocent person like in the good old days.'

There was a pause at the other end of the line. 'Be careful what you say, Rohan.'

'You can take me off the case if you want.'

'No, Rohan, you're the best person we've got, given the circumstances. Just move it along at a faster pace if you can. Clock's ticking.'

The large, grey clouds hung low and the blustery wind ruffled my hair as I walked briskly to my car. I turned on the ignition and a sheen of ice melted on the windscreen as cold air — and then hot as the engine warmed — blew from the vents. I rubbed my hands, trying to get my circulation going. Eventually, I pressed the accelerator and made my way to the south-west of the city. The morning commuter traffic was heavy as I pulled up outside what used to be my home with Faye and the children. I waited, the engine idling, the inside of the car now warm and welcoming.

A few minutes later, the front door opened, and Faye and Karan walked towards the car, my son wearing a winter coat and a big smile. I got out, hugged him and said hello to Faye. Yasmin came to the door and shouted hello. I waved to her and said I'd be in touch soon.

'Don't bring him back too late, Rohan,' said Faye.

I promised I wouldn't and wished her a good day. Karan put his *Avengers* rucksack on the back seat, I closed the passenger door after he put on his seat belt, and we drove off.

'I'm so happy to be spending the day with you today, Dad.'

'Me too, Karan. I'm really looking forward to it.'

'What about Fernando? How is he? And who's looking after him?'

I explained that Mr and Mrs Chand were looking after him for the day.

'Oh, that's good. I don't like him being alone.'

I smiled at him.

'I'm glad to be with you today. Mum and Pierre kept us awake fighting last night. Yasmin and I stay out of the way when they're like that.'

'I am sorry, Karan. What're they fighting about?'

'Not sure. Pierre usually starts shouting at Mum about something. And then she starts shouting back.'

'It'll pass,' I said, although I was concerned. 'Perhaps they're both tired. Teaching is hard and the Christmas holidays are still some way away.'

Karan shrugged. 'Why is it always like that for me and Yasmin, Dad? First it was you and Mum. Always fighting. Now it's her and Pierre.'

The comment cut through my heart. 'I'm sorry, son. You and Yasmin deserve better.'

'We really miss you.'

'I miss you and Yasmin, too.'

I placed my hand around his shoulders and squeezed. There wasn't much else I could say.

'Anyway, today we're going to London. And we'll have a fantastic time.'

'You bet, Dad. How's Anita?'

'She's good, thanks for asking.'

'Shame you don't see her much. You're happy when you see her.'

A couple of hours later, after I had parked the car at Leicester train station and we boarded the train, we arrived at St Pancras Station. I treated us to a taxi ride to the Olympia Exhibition Centre in Hammersmith. Hundreds of people milled around in the large exhibition arena as the exhibitors demonstrated the latest developments in artificial technology. Human-looking robots were interacting with the audience. Putting on virtual reality headsets we ran from dinosaurs, swam with whales and flew with an eagle. We even helped in a surgical procedure to replace a knee joint.

We stopped at a stall and bought burgers, a soft drink and some ice cream. Karan made many transient friends. They chatted for a while, exchanged comments about the technological marvels they were experiencing, then separated and moved in opposite directions. I felt happy to see my son happy. It had been a long time since I had seen him like this.

As we approached my car in the car park, Karan hugged me and said, 'Thank you, Dad. I had such a wonderful time.'

'Me too, Karan. It was lovely to spend some time together.'

'Please can we do it again soon?'

I said we would, and I desperately wanted to keep my promise. For once I agreed with Superintendent Breedon. We needed to wrap this case up as soon as possible.

It was already dark by the time I dropped Karan outside the house. Faye came to the door and we exchanged pleasantries. I decided not to say anything about what Karan had told me about the arguing. It wasn't my place. But I'd make sure to check in on both him and Yasmin more.

Back at home, Fernando was still subdued, although the Chands said he had eaten plenty and drunk copious amounts of water. They had even tried some coconut water and he liked that. He had been quite talkative, they said.

'Oh, come on, Fernando. I'm sorry,' I said to him, as he gave me the death stare from his perch. 'I didn't know what was going to happen at the Kingdom.'

He flipped on his perch, lifted his tail and pooped onto the newspaper.

My mobile rang. 'Private Caller' the screen said.

'Good evening, Inspector Sharma. Did you enjoy your day in London with your son, Karan?'

It was a voice I recognised. My stomach lurched.

'It's Duleep Shah. We met in the disused warehouse.'

'Don't ever follow me and my son again. What do you want? And make it quick.'

'Well, you're not solving the murder of Sunil Kumar quickly. The police are persecuting us needlessly. All the hassle on the streets. You should be going after those who killed our great hero. It's a pity you don't know how to do your job. You and your friends in the police have been warned. I won't be responsible for the actions of my comrades.'

The line went dead.

I woke up to my mobile phone ringing. The bedside clock showed one-thirty in the morning.

'I'm sorry, Sir,' said Angie Deacon. 'I know you told me not to ring unless it was a matter of life or death…'

I sat up, my senses on high alert.

'One of our team has been attacked,' she said, trying not to sound upset. 'I'm on my way to Glenfield Hospital now, Sir.'

'I'll see you there,' I said. I jumped out of bed, dressed quickly and dashed to the car. Thankfully, the traffic was light on the roads at this time and, since the hospital wasn't far from where I lived, I was there in about fifteen minutes.

The lawned area behind the main hospital building was bathed in a subdued light from the lampposts along the footpaths. A fine autumn mist hung in the air as I got out of my car and buttoned my winter coat.

Ben Carter and his team were already there, along with Angie. Blue and white scene-of-crime tape cordoned off part of the grounds and a large, white forensic tent had been erected.

I waved to Ben as I approached. 'Tell me,' I said.

'He was found by a nurse finishing her shift,' he said. His face was grim. His usual bonhomie absent. 'Her husband had come to pick her up and she was walking towards the car when she noticed the body on the helipad. She thought at first he was a drunk passed out.'

'Thank you,' I said. 'We'll get a formal statement tomorrow.' Ben nodded and returned to his team.

Angie and I put on our forensic suits and made our way to the tent. Nasreen stood near the body, which was sprawled out on top of the giant H on the hospital's helipad. The hands met the top of the H and the feet stopped slightly short at the other end. The familiar dark hair blew in a sudden gust of wind, the playful eyes forever closed. Angie put her hand to her mouth, suppressed a sob, and looked away. The dark, well-tailored jacket was open. The shaft of an arrow punctured the breastbone, and blood had congealed on the front of his cream shirt. A lightning bolt had been sprayed with white paint across his chest, reaching up to the top left shoulder.

'He wouldn't have taken long to die,' said Nasreen, standing next to me.

She touched my arm. 'I'm sorry,' she said. 'I gather you knew him.'

'Yes, I did. He was one of —'

I turned around at the sound of heavy, running footsteps behind me.

'Sorry I'm late, Rohan,' said Tim Lafferty, bending over and gasping for breath. 'Lisa's been struggling tonight and I had to make sure she was comfortable before leaving her. Can't wait for this baby to be born. Making our lives hell before even taking its first breath.'

'No worries, Tim.'

'Who is it?' he asked.

'It's Robert Thompson from your unit.'

Tim stared at his dead colleague for a long time and then turned away.

'I'm sorry, Tim. He was a good lad.'

'Poor Rob. He didn't deserve this. What the hell was he doing here, anyway?' Tim asked.

'He was visiting his wife, Mary,' explained Nasreen. 'She fell down the stairs, broke her leg in two places, fractured her pelvis — the orthopaedic team here had to carry out emergency surgery. She was only admitted earlier today. The doctor told me she's in the recovery room. Still groggy from the anaesthetic.'

'Shit,' I said. I wasn't looking forward to telling her that her husband had been murdered.

No one else said anything.

Nasreen broke the silence. 'The cause of death seems pretty clear. The arrow looks to have gone straight through the heart. Death would have occurred very quickly.

'And the body doesn't appear to have been dragged to the helipad — there are no obvious drag marks or signs of

166

footprints. It seems this was where he fell. The arrow was probably shot from a distance. Maybe the perpetrator was hiding in the bushes and trees over there.'

We turned to look where Nasreen was pointing. Forensic officers were already working in the area.

'The arrow is relatively short,' she continued. 'Looks to be about thirty centimetres in length, taking into account the part that's lodged inside the body. It was probably fired from a crossbow. The shaft is a standard one made from carbon fibre and aluminium. They can be easily purchased online.'

'A silent, stealthy killer,' murmured Angie. I wasn't sure if she was referring to the arrow or the murderer.

'Any idea of the time of death?' I asked Nasreen.

'The blood is still congealing so death probably occurred no more than two hours ago. I'd say eleven-thirty, or thereabouts.'

'That ties in with what the nurse said,' said Angie. 'She said she finished her shift at eleven, changed out of her uniform, then walked to the main entrance and out of the building towards her husband's car. That would make it about eleven-thirty. So Robert was killed not long before the nurse found him.'

'We have the signature,' I said. 'The *H*, the circle of the helipad and the spray-painted lightning bolt. What was Robert working on recently, Tim?'

'He was monitoring online activities by Hindu extremists, both here and abroad.'

'Shit!' I said again. I informed them of my dealings with Duleep Shah and his threats. We would need to ramp up security for every officer involved in the case.

Tim, Angie and I moved away from the forensics tent to allow Nasreen and her team to get on with their jobs.

'Angie,' I said, 'speak to the doctor and find out when we can speak to Mary, please. I'm assuming she won't be in any fit state to see anyone until tomorrow. And please ask Jamie to look at Robert's online activity, his phone records, bank statements, and so on. We need to find out why he was targeted.'

'Robert's phone was still in his pocket. We can start with that once the forensics team finish with it,' Angie replied.

'Good. And get our team to look at the CCTV footage here at the hospital, in particular the grounds around the helipad.' I looked at Tim. 'Anything else you can think of, Tim?'

Tim shook his head, his face sombre.

'Let's call it a night then,' I said. 'Go home and get some sleep. I know I need to.'

CHAPTER 25

At HQ the next day, Tim, Angie and I sifted through all the evidence we had so far about Robert Thompson's murder, but nothing new had materialised from interviews or the CCTV footage. Tim phoned Cynthia but she had no further information for us. I could see both Tim and Angie struggling through lack of sleep so in the afternoon, I decided we would finish early for the day and come back tomorrow refreshed and revitalised.

I walked in through the front door and slumped on the settee. Fernando stopped munching and looked at me from his open cage. He thrust his beak into the water tray and then stretched his neck upwards to swallow it.

'Oh, Fernando, you're so lucky. All you have to worry about is who will feed you and what you'll do next. I wish that's all I had to worry about.'

Fernando hiccupped. He seemed to be getting back to normal.

I loosened my tie, removed my jacket and walked wearily upstairs to change. A little while later, I replenished Fernando's trays with a variety of nuts and fruit and water. I defrosted some mince lamb, cooked it in a tomato sauce, and ate it with spaghetti.

It was early evening but I was shattered and ready to go to sleep. Fernando sat on my outstretched arm and I took him into the bedroom with me. He bit my right earlobe and held on.

'Oi, stop it!'

'Rohan's a bad boy,' he squawked.

'Are you referring to what happened to you at the Tropical Birds' Kingdom? Or have you been spying on me and Anita?'

He squawked as I sat him on the perch in the corner, the bedroom door open in case he wanted to go downstairs. I heard him moving about on his perch as I lay in bed, staring up at the two dodos on the ceiling. I tried not to think of Robert and his wife Mary. Whoever was behind these murders had now crossed a line by killing a police officer. I doubted they would stop there. Maybe they could come after me next … or another member of my team.

A noise woke me up. I looked at the clock. It was nine p.m. Was it my imagination? Had I heard something? It was quiet outside on the street, no voices, no cars driving past. Fernando fluttered towards me and perched on the edge of the bedside table. I stroked his head and whispered, 'Shh … stay here.'

I got out of bed and crept to the door. I heard the front door shut, furtive footsteps coming into the house. I edged slowly to the landing, wary of the floorboards creaking. My heart thumped.

The footsteps were at the bottom of the stairs. I moved back, into the shadows. The first step groaned and the person stopped. After a few seconds, the footsteps continued up. Slowly. Stealthily.

My muscles tensed. My breathing shallow. The muscles in my elbow tightened and my right hand formed into a fist.

I moved back into the bedroom. Fernando had not moved. I could see his outline in the pale light coming through the gaps in the curtains.

I stood behind the bedroom door.

The intruder advanced along the landing. An arm pushed the door open further and a figure walked in.

I slammed the door shut with an almighty crash. I raised my fist.

A woman screamed.

'Rohan! Stop!'

I froze.

'What the hell are you doing?' shouted Anita.

Fernando squawked.

I turned on the main light. 'Anita? What on earth are you doing here? I thought you were staying at the military base tonight? You didn't say you were coming back here.'

'I thought I'd surprise you. They provided me with a room, but I'd rather sleep here with you and get up early to make the drive back.'

'Well, you could have called first.'

'Do you want me to go?'

'No, no, Anita. I didn't mean that. It's great to see you. It's just… Someone I used to work with has been killed. I thought you were someone out to get me.'

'I'm sorry, I should have called first.'

She held me, gazing past my shoulder. 'God, what happened to Fernando?'

She crossed the room and picked him up.

'Oh, poor Fernando.' She stroked his head. 'Have you been starving him? He looks thin.'

I explained what had happened.

She kissed him on the head. I stared. He seemed contented.

I was pleased to see them getting along but I wondered if he was up to something.

Anit and I undressed and got into bed.

'Do we need a voyeur?' I asked, as I saw Fernando staring at us.

'Go to sleep, Rohan. You look as knackered as I feel.'

Anita woke up before me and made breakfast. When I entered the kitchen Fernando was perched on the back of one of the chairs, a chunk of pear in his beak.

I stroked Fernando's head but he jerked it away.

'Have it your way,' I replied.

He nuzzled up to Anita instead. 'I love you, Anita. I love you.' She laughed and stroked his neck.

I decided to leave early with Anita and get a head start before the others arrived at HQ. A couple of hours later the rest of the team were in, and I called a meeting in the incident room.

Tim started the briefing. 'We have discovered there were regular payments into Robert's bank account from a merchant bank in the City of London. They say it came to them from a Swiss bank account. The payments were between three and seven thousand pounds.

'Further enquiries reveal the same Swiss bank account was used to make payments to Mr Mirza, so we have a connection between two of the homicides. Unfortunately, because the Swiss are not playing ball, we can't progress with identifying the account holder.'

'CCTV showed the white van with the cloned number plates at the hospital — it can be seen driving in from a side road,' said Angie. 'It drove further on, near the trees and bushes, and out of sight of the cameras. The driver knew where they were going, and where to park. We found trampled grass and broken twigs where the sniper stood. Sadly, there was no other evidence — no footprints, no cotton thread from clothing.

'The forensics team and Dr Khan swabbed the body and clothes for DNA, which they ran through the staff database. Believe it or not, the DNA stored under Robert's name was not his.'

'Do we know whose DNA it is?' I asked.

'Yes, Sir.' She paused, cleared her throat. 'Yours.'

I blinked. 'What the hell's going on?'

'Obviously, someone swapped Robert's DNA for yours on the database,' said Tim.

'There'll be a record of which technician collected and stored the DNA when Robert was called to give his. Do we know who that is?' I asked Angie.

'Yes, Sir. His name's Mark Riley. He still works here.'

'At least we've got something to go on,' said Tim. 'Let's have a word with him, under caution.'

'Okay, go get him. Let's see what he has to say for himself. Ask a member of HR and the Professional Standards' Team to be present as well, please.'

About fifteen minutes later, Tim and Angie walked back into the room, accompanied by Mark Riley and two other HR staff.

Mark strode towards me, arm outstretched, and shook my hand. He was still wearing a white lab coat.

'Really good to meet you, Sir. Heard so much about you. What's all this about? And why the heavy brigade?' He glanced back at the two HR members.

I asked Mark to sit down, and told he was being interviewed under caution. His smile faded and he folded his arms and legs, a classic defensive posture.

I explained what we had discovered and he stared at me. I asked him why he hadn't registered Robert Thompson's sample on the DNA database?

'Am I under arrest? If so, what are the charges?'

'Yes, to the first. Obstructing a murder investigation and fabricating evidence — as starters — for the second.'

'No comment,' he replied.

'Think about it, Mark,' said Tim. 'Your career is on the line. You'll be locked up with the same criminals you helped to put behind bars. It won't be pleasant for you. If you decide to co-operate with us you could get a much lighter sentence. We, DI Sharma and I, can speak in your defence if you co-operate now.'

Mark Riley looked at Tim and then at me. He ran his tongue over his lips. 'No comment,' he said.

'Okay, have it your own way,' I said. 'Sergeant Deacon, charge him with the two offences and read him his rights. Then take him away to be held in custody. Seize all his devices and get the IT team to go through them with a fine-tooth comb. And get a warrant to search his house.'

Jamie Shriver walked in as the others were leaving.

'Sorry it's taken a while to get back to you,' he said. 'But we had to go through some complicated digital footprints on Robert's devices. We also tried to retrieve stuff he had deleted. We had a partial success. The messages he sent were encrypted, which means they're very difficult, if not impossible, to decipher. We've also been trawling through his online activities. He was heavily into online role-playing games. Made a lot of contacts that way. Sent his competitors messages through various digital platforms. But we don't really know the backgrounds of many of these people. We're still working on it.'

Jamie paused. 'Sir, can I speak to you in private, please?'

'It's all right, Jamie. You can say what you want to say in front of DI Lafferty.'

He shifted his weight from one foot to the other. 'I think it's best if I speak to you in confidence. If you don't mind.'

Tim stood up. 'I'll go see if Angie needs any help.'

I nodded.

When Tim left, Jamie told me something that shocked me to my core.

I rang Faye's doorbell after work. Footsteps came running down the stairs. The door swung open. She stared at me, surprised I had come over unannounced.

'Do you want to tell me just what the hell you were doing with Robert Thompson, Faye?'

'Rohan, what're you talking about? What are you doing here?'

'Robert Thompson, who I used to work with. You were seeing him behind my back. Sleeping with him. You betrayed me with yet another man.'

'Rohan.' Her voice trembled. 'Yasmin and Karan will soon be home. And Pierre. It's best if we sit in your car. And then I'll explain.'

'What? Tell me more of your lies?'

Her eyes filled with tears. 'It's not what it seems,' she said.

I turned around and walked to my car. She followed.

Faye sat next to me in the passenger seat. I looked away, at the house we once shared, trying not to imagine what could have taken place in our marital bed. Faye ran a hand through her hair.

'I met Robert at one of your office parties,' she said. 'I think you'd gone to the loo or were talking to someone else. He was talkative and, yes, he was good looking.'

I didn't say anything. My hands clenched the steering wheel. The knuckles tight against the skin.

'He was persistent, kept asking me for my phone number, even though he knew we were married. Eventually I agreed to take his business card.'

'And you didn't think to tell me any of this? Why the hell not, Faye?'

She took a deep breath but didn't answer my question.

'Anyway, one evening you were on a course somewhere. You'd been away for days and we weren't in a good place. I felt lonely and I decided to call him. We met in a pub, had something to eat and that was it. Nothing more.'

'That's not what the text messages say. Robert has been murdered, Faye, and we have been analysing his phone. You slept with him. And did so on a number of occasions. All the shit I had to read between the two of you. When you were supposed to be my wife. The mother of our children.'

Faye had clasped her hand over her mouth. Her breathing was heavy.

'And afterwards there was Pierre. Were there any others?'

She looked straight ahead.

'Jesus Christ, Faye! How the hell could you do this to us?'

She placed her hand on my arm. I shrugged it off.

'Don't, Faye. Please don't.'

We sat in silence for a few moments. I wanted to scream.

'I think I'll go now,' she said. 'I know you won't believe this … but I'll always cherish the love we once had, Rohan.'

'How could she do that to me, Fernando? To us? To the children? I trusted her. Even after we divorced, I rang her regularly, she was my friend. I asked her for advice. Now … now what?'

Fernando crunched a walnut in his beak and looked at me from his perch. I swigged some neat malt whiskey, having bought a bottle on my way back. I hardly ever drank spirits and I could feel the effects instantly. The television screen in my front room was a blur.

Fernando hiccupped. Or was it me?

'Bet you were there, weren't you, Fernando? When she was at it. You must've seen and heard everything.'

Fernando flew across the room and landed on my shoulder. He nuzzled my neck.

'Are we friends again, Fernando? Have you forgiven me?'

He pulled my earlobe gently.

'I love you too, Fernando… I don't blame you for wanting to come home. You open your heart to others and it gets shredded.'

I gulped some more whiskey. The amber fluid swirled in the bottom of the thick, crystal tumbler. The remnants of the ice cubes clinked against the glass.

'I don't know what to do about Yasmin and Karan, Fernando. Shall I fight for custody? Faye will definitely take me to the courts. Because I know she loves them. But is it good for them to witness her and Pierre arguing all the time? Why the hell's life so complicated?'

The television screen was one fuzzy rectangle. The voices slurred and unclear.

'Yasmin's fourteen and about to start her GCSE courses, Fernando. It would disrupt her life too much. We couldn't live here. We'd need a bigger house. And Karan starts a new secondary school soon. No, I just couldn't do that to them.'

I tried to stand up from the settee. Fernando flew back to his perch. I flopped down again.

'Why are some people such —'

'Shits,' he squawked.

I hiccupped. Two Fernandos stared back at me.

I looked at my tumbler. It was empty. I stared at the bottle. Most of the whiskey had disappeared.

'Think I'll go to bed, Fernando. I've had enough for one day. I've had enough of everything.'

CHAPTER 26

When I woke the next morning, the streetlights were still on, no daylight stole through the gaps in the curtains. My head throbbed as I struggled out of bed, fully clothed, and headed unsteadily towards the bathroom.

I swallowed two paracetamol tablets and stood under the shower for a long time. I turned the water from hot to cold, the freezing spray bringing me back to life. I shaved carefully then got dressed, putting on a navy-blue woollen suit. I went downstairs.

'Good morning, Fernando... I'm sorry for last night.'

He looked at me.

'My head hurts, Fernando.'

It was then I saw the shattered glass on the carpet. I looked up. There was a stain on the wall above the fireplace.

'Rohan's a bad boy. Rohan's a bad boy,' squawked Fernando.

'I know. I did that, didn't I? Well, do you blame me?'

I bent down, picked up the bigger shards of glass and put them into the bin. I then fetched the vacuum cleaner and vacuumed the floor a few times. I booked a taxi and a few minutes later was on my way to work. I knew I couldn't drive as I would still be over the legal limit.

'Rohan, you look like shit,' said Tim, as I walked into the incident room.

'I feel it, Tim.'

I told him the truth, not only because I'd known him a long time and considered him a friend but also because Faye's behaviour could potentially have a bearing on the case.

'Listen, Tim, I have to go see the boss — update him on the investigation. Surprised he didn't ring me last night.'

Superintendent Breedon's PA escorted me into his office, offered me a cup of coffee which I gladly accepted. He was sitting behind his large desk, the telephone receiver in one hand, a Montblanc pen in the other. Occasionally, he jotted something down on his notepad. He indicated for me to sit down.

He hung up.

'Late night, was it, Rohan? You look like death warmed up.'

'Just working hard, Sir. Like the rest of us,' I replied.

Superintendent Breedon's left eyebrow raised, making the wrinkles on his forehead dance.

'Are you sure there wasn't an innocent mix-up with Officer Thompson's DNA sample on our database?'

'No question about it. Mark Riley, the lab technician, ensured that Officer Thompson's DNA was removed from the official database. And, as you probably know by now, my sample was stored under Robert Thompson's name.'

Superintendent Breedon sat back in his chair. 'The media will have a field day if any of this gets out.'

I stared at the gleaming epaulettes on his shoulders. He cleared his throat.

'Look, Rohan, I'll be straight with you,' he said. 'We've got a few bad apples in the force. Like many forces. The Met in London has received some high-profile coverage in the wake of recent scandals.'

'You mean the racism, misogyny and homophobia, Sir?'

He sighed. 'All of this will take time, Rohan.'

'Time is something we don't have. It's a luxury only the privileged can enjoy.'

'Let the professional standards people deal with it, Rohan. I'm sure they'll weed out the perps. We need to concentrate on finding out who the hell killed one of us. Make it quick and try not to look under too many stones. We need to think of our reputation.'

'Whose, Sir? Yours or mine?'

'Wasn't your wife's number found on Officer Thompson's mobile phone?'

'Ex-wife.' The blood rushed to my face and I clenched my jaw.

'Keep me posted,' he said. I was dismissed.

I walked into the incident room at the same time as Angie and Cynthia. Cynthia explained she'd been working with the counter-terrorism unit on other matters and thought it would be good to catch up on the latest developments in our case.

'MI5 and the National Crime Agency were monitoring the activities of certain police officers,' said Cynthia. 'Not just here in Leicestershire but in other parts of the country as well. We were made aware by whistleblowers and our own intelligence network that some officers were engaged in highly unprofessional — and at times, potentially criminal — behaviour. Robert Thompson had appeared on our radar because of his spending habits — not just the purchase of expensive antiques but also his penchant for gambling. But we hadn't got further than that. Now that we've got a connection with the scientist, Jihan Mirza, and the payments being made to him from the same Swiss bank account, we think it may be possible that Officer Thompson might have been leaking information about anti-terrorist activities to his paymaster. We don't know who that is, but it's highly likely to be Islamic extremists, given the references we think are being made to

Abdul Hussain.'

Jamie Shriver knocked on the door and rushed in, carrying a laptop.

'Sorry, Sir, but this is really important. I think you should all see this.'

| He set the laptop down in the middle of the conference table and plugged it in, explaining that it belonged to Robert Thompson. The IT team had managed to recover a lot of the deleted data on the hard drive, including a video. He switched it on, and we looked at the screen on the wall.

The image showed a river bubbling downstream. The camera shook as the person holding it walked along a rutted path running along its bank. A pair of walking boots at the bottom of the screen marched purposefully along the path, which stretched into the distance. The bright blue sky and thick foliage of oak and elder splashed vibrant colour onto the landscape. A tall hill could be seen in the distance.

The walker eventually approached a clearing in the woods. At the back of the clearing was a craggy limestone cliff, scrawny bushes and vegetation growing out of the jagged rocks. Towards the base was a dark opening from which no light escaped.

The camera panned left. A large stone monolith, with a flat surface, appeared in the middle of the shot. A man was standing behind it. He was clothed from head to foot in a white robe with a red Maltese Cross embroidered on the chest. He wore a rubber mask and had a gold crown on his head. Next to him stood a woman, her white robe embroidered with silver thread. She had shoulder-length blonde hair, her nose and mouth covered by a pink veil. She looked at the man wearing the crown.

On top of the stone altar stood a golden goblet with gemstones around the rim and a flat circular base. Propped up on one side of the altar was a longsword with a thick round handle, the metal glinting in the sun's rays. On the other side was a long wooden spear with a rusty metal head. Leaning against the front of the stone was a giant hammer with a square metal head and a long wooden handle. On either side of the stone stood six men, all dressed in white robes with red crosses on their chests. Each wore a metal helmet covering their faces. Only their eyes were visible. Kneeling on the ground, dressed in white robes and facing the camera, were three women. Their blonde hair was plaited, their faces hidden by pink veils.

The man wearing the crown slowly looked up to the sky, mumbling a few incomprehensible words. Then he nodded towards the opening of the cave. Two men entered the cave and dragged out a white calf, a rope tied round its neck. It squealed and resisted, its young legs trembled. It was pulled to the altar.

'For the first time,' said the crowned man, 'we're allowing our sacred ceremony to be filmed so that others who wish to join our noble cause will know and understand what we stand for. To the rightful heirs of our beloved land, which has been sullied by generations of foreigners, we pledge its return to its people. We have been chosen by God to carry out this task and we do solemnly swear to undertake it with all our might.

'As a sign of this covenant with our Creator, we offer this calf as a sacrifice and as a symbol of our devotion to him and to our mission to return our lands to our people. This calf, which will give us greater life and strength, will be slaughtered on this, the Altar of Destiny, brought back from the Holy Land by the great Knights Templar, the ones who drove out the heathens from the Holy Land many years ago. This Altar of Destiny covered the tomb of our Lord before his resurrection.' The man bent down and kissed the edge of the stone.

The calf was trussed up by the two men and lifted onto the altar. The crowned man picked up the long wooden spear and thrust it into its chest, just below the neck. Blood collected into the goblet as it gushed out.

'The Spear of Destiny,' continued the man, 'the one thrust into the chest of our dying Lord as he was crucified on the cross by the Roman centurion, Longinus, was brought to us for protection with the Stone of Destiny. The blood will be mixed with the milk of the mother cow and, together, they will give us the strength we need for the battles to come.'

The screen went blank for a few seconds. The fourteen individuals are then seen with their backs to the cameras and the goblet is passed around from mouth to mouth.

'And now,' continued the man, 'the Sword of Vengeance will be used to butcher the calf and we will cook it on the Holy Altar. The bones will then be ground to a pulp using the Hammer of Redemption, to ask for forgiveness from our people and what has been done to them by foreigners over the centuries. Long live the Aryan nation!'

Loud cheers rang out and the screen went black.

None of us said anything.

'Bloody hell,' muttered Tim, breaking the silence. 'What on earth was Robert up to with this band of nutters?'

'We suspect he was the one filming,' said Jamie. 'We found this video on his hard drive.'

'I think that was Glastonbury Tor in the distance,' said Angie. 'The one with St Michael's Tower on top. My partner and I have been to the music festival a couple of times. The area is traditionally linked with the Isle of Avalon. You know

— Camelot, King Arthur and the Knights of the Round Table?'

My mobile rang.

'Sir,' said one of the admin staff, breathless, 'we've got a serious situation. It involves your son.'

CHAPTER 27

All eyes were on me as I ended a call with Karan's school's headteacher. I felt like I had been winded. 'There's a suspected suicide bomber at my son's school,' I choked out. 'We need to get over there. Tim, contact the bomb squad. Cynthia, Angie, please come with me.'

'Rohan,' said Tim, already on his feet. 'I'm a trained negotiator. I should come with you. Cynthia can arrange for the bomb squad.'

Tim, Angie and I rushed down the stairs and towards my Mercedes in the car park. I switched on the flashing blue lights as we sped towards Karan's school. *Please God, don't let him be near this bomber*, I kept thinking. I pressed down on the accelerator. I could hear the *chop chop chop* of a helicopter above us. My heart raced.

Oncoming cars and buildings flashed by in a blur as we raced towards the scene.

I parked in the school car park just as two armoured vans with bomb squad officers pulled up. I was handed protective gear, which I quickly put on. Angie did the same. Snipers arrived and positioned themselves on nearby vantage points. The helicopter — an air ambulance — had already landed on the school's playing field at the back of the main building and two more ambulances arrived by road. Uniformed officers surrounded the school building.

I called the headteacher. 'Mrs MacKenzie,' I said into the screen of my mobile, 'it's Inspector Sharma, can you update me on what's happening please?'

'Inspector Sharma,' she said, a little breathlessly. 'Ginny

Blanchflower, one of our teaching assistants, is in the assembly hall with a teacher, Elaine Perry, and a class of pupils. She's got a vest on with bombs attached to it. I don't know what to do, Inspector. I'm really sorry.'

'Don't worry, Mrs MacKenzie. We'll take it from here.'

There was a pause.

'No, what I mean is, I'm really sorry, but your son Karan's in the hall.'

My stomach lurched. I tried to remain calm, but my hand shook with fear.

'Just stay out of the hall; we're coming in to help evacuate the school. It needs to be done quietly, class by class. No panicking. Do you understand?'

'Yes, Inspector, I understand.'

'Can you tell me everything you know about Ginny, please?'

'She's thirty-one. Lives on her own. Has been a loyal member of staff for about eight years. She's well-liked by everyone, including the parents.'

'Have you any idea why she's doing this?' asked Tim, standing next to me. 'Sorry, Mrs MacKenzie, you're on speaker. My name's Inspector Lafferty and I'm working with DI Sharma. Is there anything you can think of that might explain this change in her behaviour?'

'Not that I know of, Inspector Lafferty. She's always cheerful at work. Oh, she did mention recently that she met someone — I think the relationship has become very serious very quickly. She hasn't mentioned an engagement, but she's been wearing a ring.'

'Do you know the name of her partner? Address?' I asked.

'No, I'm sorry. But we do have her mother's name and address as next of kin.'

'Thanks, please get the details from her records. Can you also let me have Ginny's number, please?'

'I'll get that now and meet you outside by the assembly hall.' She ended the call.

'Rohan, let me talk to Ginny,' said Tim. 'Bot not on her mobile. I think it would be better if I talk to her in person.'

'Okay, but I want you in protective gear.'

Tim shook his head. 'It would be better if she doesn't see me in full gear. It might panic her. My plan is to get everyone out of there safely.'

I looked at him. 'Okay, Tim,' I said. 'But wear your bodycam so I know what's going on. And I want you to wear a bullet-proof vest under your jacket — it'll give you some sort of protection if necessary.'

Mrs MacKenzie appeared outside the assembly hall just as a stream of children were guided out of the main school building by uniformed officers. Tim jogged across to join her.

Angie and I sat in one of the large police vans parked outside the school. I saw Mrs MacKenzie give Tim a piece of paper, presumably with Ginny's number on it. He rang the number on his phone and we watched him speak into it. He turned to give us a thumbs up before opening the hall door and entering the building.

Ginny Blanchflower appeared on the screen on my laptop. She stood on the stage with the children, who sat cross-legged in front of her. The teacher, Elaine Perry, sat with them, looking terrified

'Ginny,' said Tim, taking a few steps towards her. 'My name is Tim; we just spoke on the phone. I'm here to help you.'

'Stay back!' she shouted.

Tim stopped. Behind the children was a nativity scene, a night sky and a bright shining star of Bethlehem. Three cardboard camels stood to the sides, alongside a cut-out palm tree.

'Please Ginny, think of the children. They're scared. Why not let them go and then we can talk?'

'Nobody's going anywhere,' she said.

'Why're you doing this, Ginny? If you tell me, then maybe I can help?'

'He loved me. And they killed him.'

'Who, Ginny?' asked Tim, taking a few steps towards the stage.

Her wide eyes darted around the hall. Her face was drawn and tired, dark circles under her eyes. 'Stop right there! Don't come any nearer or I'll do it — I'll blow us all up!'

Tim stopped again. I could hear his heavy breathing through the microphone pinned to his lapel. 'Ginny, talk to me. Who was killed?'

Ginny stared at him. Her face crumpled and tears streamed down her cheeks. 'He had him killed. Because he loved me.'

'Who, Ginny? Who had who killed?'

Some of the children whimpered. Elaine Perry put her finger to her lips. I tried not to focus on Karan, dressed as one of the three wise men. He was sitting near Ginny.

'My husband, the King. My husband had him killed.'

I frowned. We were not aware she had been married.

'Who's you husband, Ginny? And why do you call him the King?'

She stared at him. 'Why, Arthur, of course. Arthur had him killed, because he found out about us.'

'Who's Arthur, Ginny?'

She pulled open her jacket. Five sticks of explosives were in each horizontal pocket. A wire dangled from the top explosive. 'Arthur Pendragon, the King. I am his Queen, Guinevere. We were married in Camelot.'

I looked at her face. The shoulder length blonde hair. The blue eyes. 'Tim,' I said into his earpiece, 'she's the woman in the video. The one in the ceremony near Glastonbury.'

Tim didn't reply.

My son Karan looked up at Ginny.

Please Karan, don't. Don't look at her. You don't know how she's going to react.

'Where's Arthur now?' asked Tim.

Ginny shrugged.

'What about your love? What was his name?'

'Lancelot.' She smiled. 'Tall, handsome — he was my knight in shining armour. He rescued me from Arthur. We were going to get married —' her smile faded — 'and now he's dead.'

'Did Lancelot have another name?'

She looked at Tim. He took another step forward.

'Please, Ginny. You want to keep his name alive, don't you? What was his real name?'

Her top lip quivered. 'Robert. Robert Thompson.'

Angie stifled a gasp next to me.

'Tim,' I whispered, 'don't tell Ginny that Robert was already married. There's no telling how she may react.'

Ginny was talking. 'I hate Arthur! Without Lancelot, I don't want to live anymore.' She moved her hand to the top wire on the explosives vest.

'No, Ginny, don't,' I heard Tim say, his voice firm. 'That won't solve anything. Please, help us and we'll arrest Arthur for you.'

Ginny hesitated. 'They'll kill me… They already made me kill Merlin,' she replied.

'Who's Merlin?' Tim asked.

'The magician. He could do anything. Arthur got him to build the tool for our salvation. But then Arthur decided

Merlin knew too much, so he had to be killed. He made me do it. We all trained to use guns in Camelot because Arthur had been a soldier. He told me to wear a *hijab* to confuse any witnesses.'

Tim moved towards her again. I could see his outstretched arm, palm facing up. 'Please, Ginny. We can sort this out. You can tell us everything. I promise you won't come to any harm.'

'Stop! Don't come any nearer. I'll pull the wire!'

Tim stopped.

'I want to go home,' said one boy and started to cry.

'Ginny, please don't do this. Think of the children. Think how their families would feel if anything happened to them?'

She ignored him. 'Arthur wanted me to wear this vest into the big Hindu temple. To set it off there so it would be blamed on the Muslims. He wanted to start a race war so that we could start rebuilding our glorious Aryan nation. He wanted me to have as many children as possible with him. Then when he found out about me and Robert, he killed him…'

'Ginny,' said Tim, 'come with me outside. We can sort this all out.'

She looked at the children sitting in front of her, as if seeing them for the first time.

'Come on, Ginny. You won't get into trouble.'

She walked to the edge of the stage and then hesitated.

'Please, Ginny,' said Tim. 'It's for the best. For everyone. And then we can deal with the person who killed Lancelot.'

Ginny bent down and put one foot over the edge of the stage and onto the floor. Then the other. Tim held out his hand towards her. She took it.

'Walk in front of me please, Ginny.'

He let her walk a few paces in front. Watching on the screen, I could feel beads of sweat on my brow. My heart raced.

As Ginny walked towards the exit, Mrs MacKenzie rushed into the assembly hall from another doorway. We could hear animated chatter, some sobbing, from the relieved adults and children.

Tim and Ginny stepped out through the door and onto the concrete playground. Tim asked her to stop. I could see our van in the distance from his camera.

'Ginny,' he said, 'you need to remove the vest now. How many buckles are there?'

'Four.'

'Okay, I'll stay here behind you. Please remove them one by one. Once you've finished, slowly place the vest onto the ground. Then we can move away and let other people deal with it. Do you understand?'

'Yes, I understand, Tim.'

It was the first time she had said his name. He was establishing a personal connection. That was good.

We could see her on the screen as she started to unbuckle the vest.

The snipers waited on their vantage points in case they needed a head shot to neutralise her.

'That's the bottom three buckles,' said Tim into the microphone. 'Now the top buckle. Wait... Shit! There's a detonator!'

Then everything happened in slow motion.

CHAPTER 28

There was an enormous explosion that almost burst my eardrums. The force of the blast shook the van, rocking it on its tyres. Bits of plaster and shards of metal rained down on the roof. A severed hand smashed into the windscreen, an engagement ring still on the finger. It slowly slid down the glass, leaving behind a long streak of blood. Angie stared at it, a horrified look in her wide eyes.

There was a large cloud of dust and smoke where Ginny Blanchflower had stood. Tim had been flung through the air and was now lying motionless on his back.

I opened the van door and rushed to him.

'No!' I shouted.

I knelt down in front of him. His eyes were closed and blood oozed from shrapnel wounds to his face. The sleeve of his jacket had been torn off, and bright red blood dripped from his arm to the ground. One leg was bent at an odd angle underneath the other. I cradled his head.

'Tim! Open your eyes. I'm here. Please, open your eyes.'

His eyelids flickered and he slowly opened his eyes. He stared at me. 'Rohan, is that you?'

'Yes, it's me. Stay with me. We'll get you to hospital.'

As I said that I heard the sound of running footsteps and then a woman's voice behind me said, 'Sir, please move aside. We need to treat this man.'

I moved away as the paramedics placed a cushion under Tim's head and got to work.

I felt numb. Somebody placed an arm around me but I pulled away and ran towards the assembly hall. The air ambulance carrying Tim rose up into the darkening sky, full of grey, menacing clouds, then banked left towards the Royal Infirmary. I burst through the hall door. I saw the children, some sitting, others clinging to members staff who had also rushed in.

'Dad! Dad!' I heard Karan shout.

I ran to him and grabbed him. Held him close.

I felt a hand on my elbow.

'Mum!' cried Karan. He let go of me and started sobbing into Faye's shoulder as she hugged him.

I ruffled my son's hair and said I'd see him before too long. That I needed to get back to work.

I rushed back to the van where Angie, her eyes red and puffy, sat waiting for me.

'Tim's in the best possible care, Angie. They'll look after him.'

She nodded. 'I hope the vest he was wearing managed to save him,' she said.

'So do I.'

I could see the number of onlookers and TV vans were increasing. I instructed my officers to keep them at bay until they heard from me or Superintendent Breedon.

'Who do you think Merlin is, Sir?' Angie asked me.

'He has to be the scientist, Mirza. But what's bugging me is why him? There are plenty of people in Afghanistan who can process opium and get it ready for transportation. Why use an Iranian scientist with a speciality in chemistry? *And* who may have been a double agent?'

'And then there's the lorry our security services were monitoring,' said Angie. 'The one from Afghanistan which went into Pakistan and then disappeared in Iran.'

My brain was desperately scrambling to put all the pieces

together. Sunil Kumar's role in all this, the stopover in Prague, the extra suitcase, the missing holdall ... the killings.

Angie's mobile rang and she answered it. 'Sir,' she said, 'you need to take this. The caller says his name's Arthur Pendragon.'

'Right, get Jamie to track this call. I'll keep him talking for as long as I can.'

Angie hurried out of the van while I put the call on speakerphone.

'Well, Sharma, we finally speak. Though your wife was doing more than that with my loyal lieutenant, Lancelot. Or Robert Thompson as you know him. What's the matter, Sharma? Couldn't keep her satisfied in bed? She had to go looking elsewhere?'

I clenched my jaw.

'Thompson was a good mole. He kept us informed of developments. But he couldn't keep it in his pants. After your wife, he started with my beloved Guinevere. Poor, misguided Guinevere, thought she was going to marry an already married man. They both betrayed me and they both knew too much. She had no idea the vest was booby-trapped.'

'And you killed Merlin, the scientist, because he knew too much as well,' I said.

'Greedy foreign bastard. We agreed a fee for his work, but he kept asking for more. I knew he was an agent for the Ayatollahs. We couldn't have done it without them.'

Although I suspected I knew the answer, I asked anyway. 'Done what, Arthur?'

'The rogue agents from the Pakistani secret service transferred uranium and plutonium to be made into a nuclear device in Iran. Once the materials were ready, they had to be transported out of south-west Iran and into Yemen, up the Red Sea and into the Mediterranean.'

'And ended up in a suitcase in Prague,' I said. 'Which was then transferred onto Sunil Kumar's jet. Other materials were also in the holdall which disappeared at East Midlands Airport but then returned a few hours later. Everything Merlin needed was now in your hands.'

'You're doing quite well, Sharma. Though Mirza only needed to arm the bomb once we had all the parts for it. He did it quite quickly in a facility in the south-east.'

I tried to keep calm. The enormity of what he was telling me was sinking in.

'And I suspect you had Sunil Kumar murdered because he also wanted more money,' I continued. 'To finance his lavish lifestyle and to kickstart his flagging career.'

'At first, he was going to sell the — let's call it the product — to some extremists here in the UK or in Europe. The rogue agents in Pakistan and some of the greedy Iranian bastards had set it all up. But when we got whiff of this consignment through our sources, we decided to make a higher bid. And your *kung fu wallah* was happy to bring it here. He did his job, got paid handsomely for it — we always honour our debts — but he didn't live long enough to enjoy the fruits of his labour.' The man laughed.

'And neither did Sunil Kumar's killer,' I said.

'Another greedy bastard,' he growled. 'He would sell his own grandmother for a few rupees. He worked closely with the rogue Pakistani agents who took cuts from the Mohammad Jahangir. He wanted a piece of the action and arranged for our consignment to be delivered to Iran. But he wanted more money when he realised the consignment wasn't going to Abdul Hussain, but to us. So he had to go, too.

'The use of the letters *A* and *H* was clever, don't you think? We scrawled them all over the world whenever any atrocities were committed. Let Abdul Hussain's extremist group take the blame, even when they didn't have anything to do with it. It suited them because of the publicity. It suited us because we hid behind it.'

'Who's the guy with the tattoo? We know him as Christopher George, but we haven't confirmed his real name,' I said.

'Oh, you mean Lucan, my faithful butler. Does everything I ask him to. And to put you out of your misery, the *A* and the *H* stand for *Aryan Heat*. The circle and the lightning bolt represent the power of our movement and the power of our wisdom.'

'And what do you plan to do next, Arthur?'

'King Arthur to you!'

'What do you plan to do, *Arthur*? Set up concentration camps for all who don't fit into your New World Order?'

'Boom,' he replied. 'Life before boom and life after boom.'

'What?'

'The trip switch has been activated, Sharma. When Ginny — God rest her soul in a million resting places — went to the ever after in an explosion of glory the trip switch was activated too. Tick, tock, tick, tock — nothing can stop it now...'

'What exactly are you talking about?'

'You have three hours before the big boom. A nitrogen bomb. It will kill most of the black and brown scum in Leicester, including you and your family, Sharma. And then we'll start repopulating the city with our glorious Aryan race. Show the world we mean business.'

'And what about all the white people who live in Leicester?'

'Collateral damage.'

The line went dead.

I rang Jamie Shriver.

'I got a trace on the mobile, Sir,' he said. 'But the signal was bounced between different servers. I lost it somewhere in the south. Sorry, Sir, I couldn't pinpoint where the caller was.'

I rang Superintendent Breedon and updated him on the situation.

'Sir,' I continued. 'Please organise all the available uniforms into small teams, and notify the army. We need them to sweep the city and beyond to find this device..'

'Okay, Rohan. I'll also keep the bomb disposal squad on standby.'

'I'm not sure how useful they'll be. They're used to defusing conventional bombs — suicide vests and roadside bombs. We need someone with experience of nuclear weapons... Can you get the Ministry of Defence to identify a scientist who can help us?'

'We're looking for a needle in haystack, aren't we Rohan?'

I ignored his comment. Instead, I said, 'Sir, we need to get the media team involved. Encourage the general public to report any suspicious packages to us. We can't allow news of a bomb to get out. It'll cause mass panic. Many could die in the stampede to get out of the city.

'Please ask our colleagues in Somerset to investigate all the caves in and around the Cheddar Gorge area,' I said. 'We think this group meets somewhere near Glastonbury. They made a mistake in letting their initiation ceremony be filmed. By the way, Sir, do you know how DI Lafferty is?'

Superintendent Breedon sighed. 'Sadly, it's touch and go. He's in the operating theatre now. They don't know if he'll make it.'

'Please let me know if ... if ... well, you know what I mean, Sir.'

I cut the connection.

Angie had climbed back into the van. I looked at her. 'Angie, if you were to plant a bomb in our city, where would you put it?'

I couldn't believe I was asking such a question.

'If I wanted to achieve maximum loss of life, then I'd put it somewhere with the greatest population density,' she replied. 'Somewhere within the city boundaries. Why do you ask?'

'It's not good news, Angie. It seems like the worst kind of bomb has been planted somewhere in Leicester and we are running out of time to find it.' Angie took a deep breath. 'Let's make a list of likely places, Sir.'

'Well, there's the Victorian clock tower in the city centre,' I said. 'An iconic structure. It's one of Leicester's defining features.'

'Then there's the King Richard III Visitor Centre,' said Angie. 'It attracts thousands of visitors every year. And the National Space Centre — another popular museum. Then there's the university buildings, the De Montfort Hall, the railway station and the Royal Infirmary, among others.'

'Angie, it could be anywhere.' My heart sank. 'Let's try and narrow it down. The attack is racially motivated so the bomb has probably been placed in an area with high numbers of black and brown people. Highfields, the Belgrave Gate and Melton Road areas. Narborough Road and the surrounding areas, including our headquarters. The area to the east of the city, around Green Lane Road and Uppingham Road. Or perhaps the suburbs of Oadby and Wigston, though they don't have the same concentration of people of colour as the others I've mentioned.'

'Still a big area to cover for our teams, Sir.'

I drummed my fingers.

My colleagues around the school were still working away at the scene, the blue and white exclusion tape cordoning it off.

The onlookers had disappeared. Nobody was aware of the catastrophe about to befall the city. I tried not to think of Karan and Yasmin, or of my parents. Or poor Fernando. I had to remain calm.

'Angie,' I said, 'let's go and speak to Mark Riley. He's the only contact we have with this group, *Aryan Heat*. Let's see if we can get anything out of him.'

I placed a call to the prison governor at Leicester Prison as my car raced along the dual carriageway. A steady drizzle had begun to fall and the automatic windscreen wipers waved slowly at me. It felt like a last farewell.

'Sir,' I said to the governor as oncoming headlights blurred, 'this is critical. I'm on my way to the prison now. Please have the guards open the gates for us on arrival. And have Mark Riley ready to be interrogated.'

CHAPTER 29

The big gates swung open as the flashing blue lights on my car alerted the guards. Angie and I ran towards the main block of the prison.

I met the governor and we were shown into a private room. Mark Riley smirked as Angie and I rushed in, both breathing heavily. We sat down opposite him across the interview desk.

'Mark,' I said, 'Ginny Blanchflower is dead.'

The smirk left Mark's face. 'You're lying.'

'She was wearing a suicide vest which Arthur had specially made for her. He told her to go to a Hindu temple, but she had other ideas when she found out Arthur had Robert Thompson killed. She was going to detonate the vest at the school where she worked, but fortunately she had a change of heart. As she was pulling the vest off, Arthur detonated it remotely. Not much is left of her.'

Riley shook his head. 'Arthur wouldn't do that. He loved her.'

I scrolled down my mobile screen and brought up the BBC News app. I showed him the 'Breaking News' article: '*One member of staff has been killed at an explosion at a local primary school in Leicester. She was a much-loved member of the school community. Another unidentified man has been seriously injured but his condition has not been confirmed by authorities. The cause of the blast remains unknown.*'

'DI Lafferty got caught in the blast. We don't know if he's going to make it. That means we can charge you with conspiracy to murder. And further charges under the Prevention of Terrorism Act unless you want to tell us what's going on.

'We know Arthur Pendragon — or whatever his real name is — was a soldier, but I need more information. What's his real name? Which regiment was he in? Where was he stationed? Where does he live?'

'I know nothing about him,' Riley said.

'Mark,' I pleaded with him, 'Arthur is planning to set off a massive explosion. Nuclear. It'll kill thousands. Including your friends and family. Is that want you want? Is that how you want your life to end? And theirs?'

He stared at me.

'Mark... Please. You're one of us. We both work for the police service.'

'I don't work for anybody anymore.'

'The bomb will detonate in about two hours,' I continued. 'You'll die too. Is that what you want?'

He didn't reply.

Angie clenched her fist on the table in frustration.

I tried again. 'Our colleagues in Somerset are already looking for Pendragon in the caves round Glastonbury. He and the others will be caught. And when he is, he'll sell you out — you and Lucan will take the rap for murder.'

'How d'you know about Lucan?'

'Arthur told me about him. How else would I know? Mark, please, you've got to help us. Many innocent people will die.'

Riley's chair grated on the floor as he pushed it back. He stood up and said to the guard, 'I'm ready to go back to my cell.'

Angie and I raced back to the car. The drizzle had turned into a steady shower. I switched on the engine and ran my fingers through my hair. Angie looked at the screen on her mobile.

'We've got less than two hours,' she said.

I wondered whether to ring Superintendent Breedon to see if he had found a nuclear scientists to help us. But what good would that do unless we found the device?

'Sir?' I heard Angie say.

She was looking out of the passenger window, through the rain. 'One of the prison guards is flashing his torch. He's running towards us.'

'Inspector Sharma,' the man shouted through the car window, out of breath. 'He's agreed to talk. Mark Riley ... he says he'll speak to you.'

I opened the car door and ran back. Angie was on my heels.

We went back to the same room. Mark Riley stood next to the desk.

'Okay, Inspector Sharma, I'll help. I don't want to die in this pit. I'll tell you what I know. Which isn't a lot because Arthur only informed people on a need-to-know basis. I had no idea about Ginny and I'm sorry about DI Lafferty.'

'Anything, Mark. Anything to help us locate the device. But please hurry. We're running out of time. The bomb will explode in...'

'One hour fifty minutes,' said Angie, looking at her watch.

Mark Riley shifted his weight from foot to foot. 'I don't know much about Pendragon. But he once let slip that his Christian name was "Les". And one of the others once referred to him as "Mr Smith". I have no idea if that's his real name, but he was annoyed the other person had used it."

'Where does he live, Mark?'

'Somewhere around Leicester. But I have no idea where. He often boasted of his army service in Iraq and Afghanistan. I think he was in the infantry.'

'Any idea what he does now? Or has done recently?' I asked.

'He once complained he'd injured his back moving a patient from a hospital bed to a wheelchair.'

'Is he a nurse?' asked Angie.

'No idea. He didn't display any particular medical knowledge.'

'Where did you meet for your initiation ceremonies?'

'Mostly around Cheddar Gorge. In and around caves that are not disturbed. Some that nobody's ever been to, or know exist. One of our knights is a farmer and he lets us use his land for training exercises, target practice, orienteering, that sort of thing. Some also meet in a disused coal mine in Nottinghamshire. They use generators for electricity inside the tunnels. Got plenty of food and other essential items for survival. For the beginning of the New World Order. Unfortunately, they killed a white boy who stumbled upon their plans in the coal mine. I heard the others talking about him. They buried his body in the mine.'

Angie and I glanced at one another.

'That's all I know. We were sent messages individually. Nobody knew much about what someone else was doing. I had no idea about this bomb.' He shrugged. 'I don't want the blood of thousands on my hands.'

'Thanks, Mark. If you think of anything else, please let me know. Just tell the governor you need to speak to me urgently.'

We raced to my car. Angie dived into the seat next to me.

'Angie, if this "Les Smith" is a nurse or porter, then we've got three hospitals: the Royal Infirmary across the road, the General in the east of the city and Glenfield to the north. Smith could be working in any one of them.'

She glanced at her watch. 'We've got an hour and thirty-five minutes.'

I rang the office of the chief executive at each hospital. No reply.

We raced to the Royal Infirmary. Rushing into the main entrance, I explained to the receptionist who we were and asked to speak to any senior manager on duty who could help with a staffing matter.

She made various phone calls and a few minutes later, a young man in his late twenties walked briskly towards us. He introduced himself as Euan Anderton. I shook his hand and asked if we could talk in a quiet room.

'Mr Anderton, this is really important. We need to track down a man we think is a nurse or hospital porter. Most probably in one of our three hospitals…'

He looked at me, wide-eyed. 'Inspector Sharma, the Trust employs thousands of support staff across its hospitals. Finding one individual would be like looking for a needle in a giant haystack. And I just don't have the staff at this time of night to go through the records at *this* hospital, never mind the other two.'

'Please, Mr Anderton. Start with the records here. We'll have to work out what to do about the other two.'

'I can access the HR records, but you'll have to give me a bit more information to go on.'

'Try Les or Leslie Smith, hospital porter, army background.'

He turned on the computer at the desk and typed in his password.

I drummed my fingers on the desk. Angie kept looking at her watch.

He typed rapidly on the keyboard, scrolled down, pressed the Enter key, clicked, scrolled, squinted, and then repeated the process, all the while murmuring, 'No… no … no…'

I looked at Angie. She flashed her watch at me.

We had one hour and ten minutes left.

A sudden thought occurred to me.

'Hang on a minute, Angie. Maybe Smith was working there at the time Robert Thompson was killed.'

Then another thought struck me.

I hit speed dial on my phone and told Jamie Shriver to contact the mobile phone companies who use the transmission towers near the school. 'Ask them to trace any unknown signals from about the time of the explosion,' I said. I also asked him to get over to Glenfield Hospital as quickly as possible with a team and electronic scanning equipment.

'Mr Anderton,' I said, 'please ring your colleagues at Glenfield Hospital. Ask them if a man named Les Smith works there. And please hurry.'

Euan Anderton picked up his mobile and rang the number of an HR officer.

'Ada, I know you're busy, but this is a police matter. Can you access the HR records and see if we've got a Les or Leslie Smith working on the hospital estate. Probably as a porter. Army background. Yes, you can call me back.'

The minutes ticked by. No return phone call. My fingers drummed. The clock on the wall ticked.

After what felt like a lifetime, Euan's phone buzzed. He listened, then hit the disconnect button.

'Yes, Inspector, we do have a Mr Smith.'

'Send me the link to his details on my phone.' I gave him my number.

Angie and I raced from the building.

CHAPTER 30

My car hurtled down the dual carriageway to the north of the city, blue lights flashing. Windscreen wipers going at full speed as the rain continued to fall heavily.

'It's a perfect job for someone like Smith,' I said to Angie. 'He can wander round the hospital grounds without attracting any attention. Possibly pushing a patient in a wheelchair or an empty hospital bed. He can access all areas. A hospital is a perfect place to hide a bomb. Not far from the city and some of the areas he would want to target. Including the Golden Mile. Where I live.'

'Sir, how on earth do we find the bomb?'

I thought for a moment. I rang Superintendent Breedon and asked him to send in the bomb disposal team. He informed me that he and the Chief Constable were still trying to get hold of a nuclear weapons' specialist, one near enough to be of help.

As my car fishtailed into the main car park and came to a halt, one of Jamie's vans screeched to a halt not far away.

Jamie ran towards me through the rain. Other cars and vans containing uniformed and plainclothes' officers arrived, joined by five armed response units. I told all of them to remain on standby.

Jamie's phone rang. He answered it. When he finished the call, he said, 'Sir, one of the mobile phone companies has just got back to me. An unidentified signal was picked up by their engineers who were working nearby. The signal emanated from just outside the school — maybe the bomb in the suicide vest — after it had been activated. Instead of being bounced to another transmitter it was directed into the fibre optic cable network and ended up in the server at this hospital. They thought it was a cyber-attack at first but because the hospital didn't report anything, they didn't follow it through.'

'Jamie, could the signal be used to communicate with another device?'

'Yes, that's easily achieved through the hospital's Wi-Fi network.'

I wiped the rain from my face.

Then it hit me. This was what Jihan Mirza's wife had referred to when I met her. Something Jihan was doing *for* and not *in* Leicester. A signal that could be identified by the police or a phone company. A signal on a different frequency to everything else. If he was double-crossed, he knew this signal would lead to the device, and a trail to follow would be identified. This information also confirmed we were at the right hospital.

I looked at my watch. We had fifty-five minutes left. I gazed at the sprawling hospital grounds. There were at least a hundred cars in the car park, and hundreds of staff and patients, many different buildings housing different departments, including operating theatres, the cardiac unit, chemotherapy services and the pathology department. Unmarked bomb disposal vans drove into the car park. I instructed them to wait with the other units until we had identified the location of the device.

Angie, Jamie and I ran into the hospital and were met by the senior manager in charge, a woman named Harriet, whom Euan Anderton had alerted. We were led into a side room. I asked Harriet to place the hospital on maximum security alert, to reassure everyone these were just precautionary measures and for staff to notify us of any suspicious packages or devices. Finally, and most importantly, all staff were to go about their usual routines. 'Obviously, we don't want to panic the staff and patients, Harriet,' I said.

'If you were a porter,' I asked Angie and Jamie after Harriet had left, 'where would you hide a bomb? One that's not too large, not too small, but capable of being hidden?'

'Obviously, nowhere crowded, like a ward or a laboratory, or an operating theatre, or any of the offices,' said Jamie.

'A porter would have ready access to the ambulance bay — but that's too busy. Could be one of the cupboards with all the cleaning equipment?' suggested Angie.

'There must be hundreds of those,' responded Jamie.

'What about the building where the gardening equipment's kept? Or with the emergency generators, one of the toilets, the rooms for the site maintenance staff...'

'I'm not sure,' said Jamie. 'If the bomb has been placed near any electronic machinery here at the hospital — I'm talking about X-ray machines, scanners, nuclear medicine, orthodontics, electronic monitors — then they might confuse the signal — if there is one. Our scanning equipment may not pick up a particular signal. But what kind of signal are we looking for, Sir?'

I stared at him. I hadn't given it much thought. Do armed nuclear devices emit beeps? Radiation? Any kind of signal? 'Anything out of the ordinary, Jamie. I've no idea at this stage.'

The hospital manager reappeared.

'Harriet, please send out a message to all of your housekeeping staff. Ask them to search inside cupboards and toilets for any unusual items. Ask the ward staff if any visitors have left anything suspicious behind. Ask your site maintenance people to search everywhere. Grounds, sheds, garages, in the trees, shrubs...'

'I'll do what I can, Inspector. But some of the ground staff don't work at night.'

'Please, Harriet, just ask as many as you can to search. It's urgent. Plus ask office staff to do the same for their areas. My officers will be searching too. Ring me on my number if anything's found.' I gave her my business card.

She rushed out.

'Angie, ask the plain clothes officers to go to the electricity generator areas and the IT suite. Use the uniforms, too, but ask them to keep their presence low key. We don't want to worry people unnecessarily.

'Jamie, get your scanning equipment and let's sweep some areas. We'll start with the X-ray department and nuclear medicine.'

My watch indicated that we had thirty-five minutes to find and disarm the device. My hands trembled.

Jamie ran out and soon returned with some hand-held scanning equipment. As we passed through the hospital I thought I heard the rotor blades of a helicopter slowing down, ready to land on the helipad. Most likely a seriously ill patient being transferred here.

We ran from area to area. Searched waste bins, looked in toilets. Nothing. I asked the other teams over the radio where they were, if they'd come across anything. The grounds were being covered. Some of the officers were scouring the car park. All reporting nothing.

Twenty-five minutes to go.

Angie caught us up. I paused to think. What does a porter do without arousing too much suspicion? Where can they go in and around the hospital?

'Angie,' I said, 'the mortuary's being searched, isn't it?'

'Should be,' she replied. 'Let me get an update.'

She spoke into her radio.

'Searched by plain clothes team just a few moments ago. Nothing, Sir.'

A porter would help transfer corpses to the mortuary. Many people would actively avoid such a place — too morbid. Apart from an attendant or two, I imagined it would be very quiet there. Deathly quiet.

'Did they check inside the refrigerators? Inside the body bags?'

'I assume so,' she replied. 'I'll check.'

I watched the second hand on my watch move round — seemingly far quicker than normal — as Angie asked the question.

'They looked inside each compartment, but didn't look under the shrouds.'

I rang the hospital manager. 'Harriet, can you find out if Les Smith transported any deceased patients to the mortuary over the last few days please? I'll stay on the line.'

I drummed my fingers against my thigh.

'I just checked his duty rota with the team leader. The answer is yes, he did.'

I lunged through the doors of the mortuary. The cold air made me shiver as I stood in front of the rows of square, stainless steel doors — a dead body behind each one. The mortuary attendant stared at us. Angie flashed her badge at him. I opened the first door and pulled out the tray, which glided out smoothly on wheels. I lifted the shroud to reveal an elderly man with a shrivelled face, his eyes closed. There was nothing else there. Jamie and Angie did the same, pulling out a tray, taking a good look at the corpse and the refrigerated compartment itself.

I pulled the drawer on the top left. My hands were freezing.

The body was covered from head to toe. I flung back the shroud. No body. Just sheets and towels. I stared inside the dark compartment. At the back was a metallic object with a small, flashing red light.

My heart raced as I ordered the mortuary attendant to leave. Slowly, I pulled out the steel tray and clambered on top. Edging my way into the cold and claustrophobic tunnel, I reached for the device. My hands slipped. I reached again and slowly pulled the device out along the metal tray. Lifting it with both hands, I slipped down off the tray and placed it carefully on the mortuary table.

My breathing heavy from the exertion, I looked at the device. It was almost a metre long and must have weighed about ten kilos. A large round shining ball was welded into the middle of a long metal frame. On top of the shining ball a small red light blinked and next to it a rectangular window flashed white digital numbers on a black background. We had nine minutes and fifty-four seconds. *Fifty-three, fifty-two, fifty-one...*

Jamie and Angie stared at the clock and then their frightened eyes found mine.

'Now what?' asked Angie.

The door burst open.

It was a member of the bomb disposal team wearing a brown boiler suit with body armour and carrying a large silver metal suitcase. Next to him was a tall woman in her mid-thirties, with dark hair and olive skin, dressed in blue jeans and a cream-coloured fleece. She was carrying another silver metal case with ridges on the cover. It was edged in black rubber.

'I'm Dr Leila Qureshi,' she said in an American accent. 'Weapons specialist based at our airbase in Northamptonshire. We just arrived here by helicopter. Your people from MI5 and MI6 filled in my commander about what's going on. I was the nearest available person. Hopefully, Daniel here and I can deal with this.'

She looked at the device on the mortuary table. Placed the metal case down next to it. She asked Daniel to put his case on another table nearby. She opened her case, stared at the metal frame and the shining ball in the middle. The digital clock blinked eight minutes and fifty-one seconds…

'Daniel, get the electric drill and the fibre optic cable. Hurry!' she said. 'And plug in all the equipment we need. Transformer, monitor screen and the rest.'

Daniel opened the larger of the two metal cases, unloaded the equipment requested, plugged square boxes into various electrical sockets. They came alive with numerous flashing lights. He then placed a bright light next to the device. Leila Qureshi ran her fingers over the spherical dome.

'Looks like steel. Probably got a uranium casing inside. For the pit.' Daniel nodded and handed Dr Qureshi a pair of large metal cutters which she used to snip the metal frame from the top of the sphere.

'This baby's bigger than any I've ever seen. If it's a neutron bomb — a dirty bomb — it'll have an enhanced radiation warhead,' she said, as she picked up the electric drill. 'Got a diamond tip. Should be able to drill through the steel and the casing under it. Pass me a mask.'

Seven minutes and thirty-five seconds…

The drill whirred, Daniel looked on, running his tongue along his bottom lip. My hands were clammy. Dr Qureshi concentrated, using the remnants of the metal cage as a support for her arms.

The drill bit slipped and scratched the outer surface of the sphere. She quickly pressed it back into the hole which was getting deeper. She carried on for a few more seconds. She slowed the rotation of the drill bit and used a long thin brush to move the dust carefully onto a piece of brilliant white paper.

She looked at Daniel and mumbled through the mask, 'Fetch me the torch.'

He handed her a powerful electric torch. She pointed it at the hole and looked at the white paper. She filtered the dust into a small glass jar and took off her mask.

'The dust is a mixture of steel filings and silvery-grey metal dust. The pit must be made of uranium.'

Six minutes, twenty-five seconds…

'Daniel, get me the fibre-optic cable and the monitor.' She looked at me and said, 'I need to look into the device, like a doctor doing a colonoscopy. I'm not sure how it's constructed. It could have a tamper switch. If it does and I get it wrong… Well, then we'll all be meeting our respective makers.'

Daniel gave her a long thin cable which was plugged into the monitor screen. Dr Qureshi inserted the brightly lit end into the hole in the sphere. Her hands trembled.

The monitor screen burst into life. Angie, Jamie and I had no idea what we were looking at as Dr Qureshi said, 'This baby is a nasty piece of work. It's a thermonuclear weapon. The primary here I've just bumped into has a neutron reflector. There's a lot of wiring inside so I need to be careful.'

She moved the cable to the left and to the right, pulled it out slightly and pushed it back again, careful not to touch anything else. The light at the end looked like the searchlight of a submersible in the deep ocean.

'Each device has many different designs and it has to be disassembled in the same way it was constructed. I've no idea how this was made. One wrong move on my part and…'

Five minutes and five seconds…

A trickle of sweat ran down my back. Angie's terrified face

turned towards me. I tried to smile.

'Another reflector,' Leila said. 'The first could be beryllium and this one here could be enriched uranium. There's plenty of Styrofoam. There'll also be lithium deuteride, though I can't easily see it. There's some more stuff in there. Maybe plutonium. Must be fissionable material to produce high levels of radioactive fallout. We need all those components for an almighty nuclear reaction. If I am right, then this baby will emit more than ten times the amount of neutron radiation compared to a fission bomb. Everyone in a radius of several miles will be killed.'

Four minutes and forty-three seconds...

Dr Qureshi looked at the monitor. A muscle under her left eye twitched.

'I'm not sure what to do. There's enough space inside the pit — the ball — to drown it in acid. To destroy the wiring and other parts of the live components. But if there's a tamper switch then...'

Four minutes and twenty-three seconds...

The motor in one of the fluorescent lights buzzed. Beads of sweat shone on Angie's forehead and yet she shivered, rubbing her hands on each arm, trying to keep warm.

Dr Qureshi spoke. 'There's no time to ask any of my colleagues for further advice. There's only one other thing I can think of. But it's not been properly tried or tested... Daniel, get me the two jars of steel powder and the steel wire.'

Three minutes and forty-nine seconds...

Daniel handed her the jars from the bigger of the two cases.

She placed the jars on the mortuary table next to the device.

'Funnel, please.'

Daniel handed her a thin plastic funnel with a long, tapered end. It would not fit into the hole she had made. She picked up the drill and widened the edges of the hole. She carefully pushed the end of the funnel into the hole again.

'I don't want to disturb the electronic mechanism,' she said, as she pressed it down slowly.

As she did this, Daniel poured some of the steel powder into a test tube and handed it to her. Her hand shook as she poured some of it into the funnel. The fine steel powder glided down through the funnel and into the steel ball. Daniel handed her another test tube and she did the same again, her tongue protruding slightly from her mouth as she concentrated.

Two minutes and eleven seconds...

As she poured the steel powder into the funnel, she said, 'I'm trying to stuff the pit. Every pit in a nuclear weapon, the hollow sphere made of plutonium or enriched uranium, has a tiny tube through it that allows the tritium to be fed inside it. If steel powder or a steel wire is fed though this small tube, we can stuff the pit with tangled wire and its powder. Meaning the pit can no longer be compressed enough by the explosives surrounding it to sustain a nuclear chain reaction. The weapon cannot go off.'

One minute and seventeen seconds...

'Daniel, pass me some steel wire.'

Dr Qureshi inserted the end of the wire into the hole and pushed it all the way inside, including its end. And then another, as far as it could go.

Fifteen seconds...

The digital clock did not stop. Dr Qureshi looked at me. She looked at the others.

Ten, nine, eight...

I looked at Angie and Jamie and wondered if I'd ever see them again. I thought of my children. My mother and father. Fernando. I said a silent prayer. I thanked them for being a part of my life. I hoped Tim would get better. And thought of the futility of that last sentiment.

...four, three, two...

There was a blue spark. A thin flame shot through the hole in the ball. A fizzing sound. Sparks flew. An acrid smell. Smoke burst the hole.

A dark blue cloud engulfed us.

Angie grabbed my hand and screamed.

CHAPTER 31

The Diwali lights twinkled bright along the Golden Mile, celebrating their victory of good over evil. The thousands of lights in the shapes of stars and circles and diamonds, joined together with invisible cables, adorned the brick walls of the shops. Long, drooping necklaces of bright, shining bulbs hung from lampposts along each pavement, and along the pedestrian refuges in the middle of the road.

The Golden Mile was busy as traffic from the school run, buses, vans, and cars crawled along the wide road. The intermittent horn blared, an old diesel engine clacked, and thick plumes of exhaust fumes poisoned the air. People in thick winter clothes peered into shop windows and inside doors, waving to faces they recognised, while others eyed up the bright yellow *pendas*, the cream-coloured *barfi*, the orange *jalebi* and the *ladoos* in the cafes and the sweetmeat shops. The vegetarian restaurants had been open since eleven o'clock in the morning and people of all shapes, size and colour sat and ate in them. The familiar laughter, the friendly banter in Gujarati, Punjabi, Urdu and English was heard again.

A sudden gust of cold wind ruffled my hair and I pulled up the collar of my winter coat. I looked down to make sure the bouquet of colourful flowers standing in one corner of my shopping bag had not been crumpled. I walked along the road, relieved that life seemed to have returned to some sort of normality as an uneasy peace, a temporary truce, settled over the city like a warm, comforting blanket. The Hindu new year seemed to promise a new beginning and Christmas, a time of goodwill, was not far away.

I entered a cafe serving Indian snacks and *masala* tea. The cardamom, cloves and cinnamon in a hot, sugary and milky cup of tea would warm me up. I ordered a plate of *pakoras* and sat at a quiet table in the corner, a television set nearby. I made a phone call.

'Are you enjoying your time off *in lieu*, Angie?'

She replied she was.

'I don't blame you for screaming, so please don't feel bad about that. I was about to do the same but you beat me to it.'

She laughed.

'Thankfully, whatever Leila Qureshi did, it worked,' she said. 'I really thought we weren't going to make it.'

'So did I, Angie. And she took the device with her. Dare say our scientists and spooks will have a good look at it. See how it was constructed, how far the technology for such things has advanced in the Middle East. It's not our problem. Not anymore.'

I wished her well and told her to have a good, long rest. I was going to do the same.

My *pakoras* arrived and I sipped the hot tea between mouthfuls of crispy food. I retrieved the latest copy of *Private Eye* from my bag and flicked through it.

I stopped and looked at the television screen.

Sky News was reporting a 'breaking news' story.

'*...and here's Superintendent Breedon of the Leicestershire Constabulary to explain further:*

'*In conjunction with our colleagues in Nottinghamshire and in the West Country, we raided two sites that have been used for some time for extremist activities. These sites were reported to us by vigilant members of the public who saw suspicious activities late at night at a disused coalfield in north Nottinghamshire and near some caves in Somerset. A large number of weapons and ammunition was recovered. We arrested a few individuals, including Leslie Smith, who is thought to be the leader of the group. Sadly, we also found the body of a young man named Zac Cavendish, who was reported missing by his parents to our colleagues in Nottingham in September. We do not believe he was part of the extremist group and everything points to the possibility he was an innocent victim. Our enquiries are still ongoing...'*

'Is this linked to the explosion at the primary school in Leicester where a member of staff was killed?'

'We cannot say for certain at this stage. But under my leadership and direction, and the continuing support of the Chief Constable, I believe we have apprehended all the known criminals in this rather complex case. Much of it is to do with the laundering of money from drugs...'

I looked away, gulped down my tea, and strolled out to my car.

The food and the tea had warmed me up but the icy wind made my eyes water. I drove off as the mist on the windscreen cleared and made my way along the dual carriageway, in the opposite direction from my house. After fifteen minutes, I arrived at my destination, parked the car, and walked into the building. I was apprehensive as I climbed a flight of stairs and pressed a buzzer. Lisa, Tim's wife, welcomed me in as I gave her the flowers. She was still heavily pregnant.

She hugged me clumsily and we eventually separated. She told me she was pleased I had found the time to come round and pointed me towards another door.

Tim, lying on the hospital bed, smiled. Despite the swelling, his eyes sparkled. 'Rohan, you old devil, how're you?'

I rushed over and hugged him. I felt him wince and let go.

'Sorry, Tim, didn't mean to hurt you. I'm so glad to see you on the mend.'

Tim looked at me and then stared down at his body. Both legs were in plaster and his face was covered in scratches and stitches. Parts of his scalp had been shaved for stitches but some thick black hair had sprouted back.

'These are the bits you can see, Rohan. Got a long scar across my stomach, too. Had a few internal injuries caused by the shrapnel.'

'I'm so glad to see you again, Tim. Thought you were a gonner.'

'Yeah, don't remember much of it. Going to take a fair old time to get back to normal again.'

'I'm sure. But you're going to be a dad soon. How wonderful!'

His eyes welled up. 'I didn't want it to be like this, Rohan. For my son to see me like this. Not being able to help Lisa.'

I tried to smile. There wasn't much I could say. I put an arm on his shoulder. 'It'll work out in the end, Tim. Please don't think too much about it. Won't be long before you'll want to come back to work.'

He looked at me. The screen monitoring his vital signs sounded an occasional bleep. 'I don't think that's going to happen, Rohan. Lisa doesn't want me to go back. I'm not sure I want to, either. I want to spend time with my son. Watch him grow up. I'll try to get a desk job, nine to five and all that. Maybe even back at HQ. But my days on the streets are over.'

I said I didn't blame him, we made further small talk, and I said I'd be back to see him before too long.

As I drove home, I rang my children. After the usual chit-chat about school, Yasmin said, 'Dad, me and Karan are really looking forward to going on holiday with you. For Christmas and the New Year. Can we go somewhere nice and warm? Like the Caribbean or, well, anywhere warm and sunny.'

I had spoken to Faye recently. I explained the kids were unhappy about the situation with her and Pierre and that it was affecting their mental well-being. She had agreed that they could stay with me for the holidays. My relationship with her had changed forever, after yet another betrayal. I tried not to think about how many other men there had been.

'Yes, darling,' I replied to my daughter, 'I'll make sure we go somewhere warm and sunny. Where we can swim with dolphins and eat wonderful food.'

'Will Anita be coming with us, Dad? We like her.'

'I asked but she's working abroad for three months with the army.'

What I didn't say is that both Anita and I had decided our relationship was difficult to maintain over a long distance. She didn't want to leave her job — not that I asked her to — and I didn't want to leave mine — not that she asked me to. Sometimes things were just not meant to be. Like the time of the Hindu and Gregorian New Years, it was time for a fresh beginning. I would tell the children and my parents about Anita when it felt right to do so.

I parked the car, caught a glimpse of fading *rangoli* patterns on the pavement, and walked into my cold front room, carrying my heavy bag of groceries. I lit the gas fire and turned up the thermostat for the central heating. Fernando squawked, fluttered and rested on my shoulder.

'I love you, Rohan. I love you.'

'I love you too, Fernando.'

It was late evening, I prepared some vegetable samosas, and grilled chicken wings marinaded in a thick tandoori paste. I muted the television set and listened to music on the smart speaker while savouring my food. I looked at Fernando as he preened his feathers on his perch. His eyes drooped as 'Albatross' played on the speaker. His head moved up and down.

I didn't have the heart to say it and wondered how much he'd understand, but I said it anyway. 'I'm really sorry, Fernando. But Anita's not going to come here anymore. You won't see her again.'

He opened one eye and gave me the death stare.

'I am sorry. But we just couldn't carry on like that anymore.'

He opened his other eye, turned his back towards me, lifted his tail and pooped.

'Can't say I blame you,' I said with a sigh.

Despite much coaxing, he wouldn't turn around.

I reflected on recent events in my home city. I thought of the futility of the actions of some people. We breathe the same air, eat the same food, wear more or less the same clothes, and we exist on this fragile planet for a brief period of time. Yet many want to kill each other. For what? It was beyond me. Why not leave a positive mark inside the hearts of everyone we come across instead?

Fernando twirled on his perch. He stared at me.

'Fernando, why are some people —'

'Shits!' he squawked.

'No, Fernando. I was going to say nuts.'

He raised his wing.

A NOTE TO THE READER

Dear Reader,

Thank you taking the time to read the third DI Rohan Sharma thriller, *The Right Time to Die* and I sincerely hope you enjoyed it as much as the first two books in the series, *The Dance of Death* and *Shattered Dreams*. I grew up in Leicester and I still visit friends and family regularly from my current home not too far away. I am proud to call it my home city and, like many other communities there, my father moved to Leicester from Kenya. My mother and the rest of my siblings followed him several years later. As many of you will know, Leicester is a vibrant and thriving city, and an important part of its history and changing nature is reflected in the area of the Golden Mile to the north. This is an exciting world, and I wanted DI Rohan Sharma to be located there because it is his spiritual and cultural home, despite him having lived in other parts of the world and in other cities.

As regular readers in the genre will know, there are not many protagonists who are from Rohan Sharma's background. I wanted to write about an ordinary detective of South Asian origin who is trying to make a positive difference within his home city. But he also faces particularly unique challenges because of his background, which he tries to overcome. I also wanted to develop a complex character who straddles a multi-dimensional world, and this is reflected in many aspects of his life.

I undertake an enormous amount of research with each book I write, including forensics, geography and history. For those of you who are interested in the issues covered in *The Right*

Time to Die, I read the following to help me understand better the politics of the contemporary world, both here in the UK and further afield:

The Rage: The vicious Circle of Islamist and Far-Right Extremism by Julia Ebner

Going Dark: The Secret Social Lives of Extremists by Julia Ebner

Hitler's Priestess by Nicholas Goodricke-Clarke

The Occult Roots of Nazism by Nicholas Goodricke-Clarke

The Nazis and the Occult by Paul Roland

The Unending Game by Vikram Sood

The New Spymasters by Stephen Grey

Hope Not Hate publications detailing extremist activities in the UK and other parts of the world.

In addition, there are many credible sources online and I was always careful to double-check the information provided.

I try to ensure that procedures for homicide investigations are accurate, but I have taken a few liberties with this novel in the belief that police procedures should respond to an evolving situation and not be set in stone.

Finally, if you enjoyed reading *The Right Time to Die* I would be grateful if you could spare a few moments to post a positive review on **Amazon** and **Goodreads**. You can **follow my author page on Facebook** for updates on my books.

Many thanks to you all for your continued support and encouragement.

C. V. Chauhan

Sapere Books is an exciting new publisher of brilliant fiction and popular history.

To find out more about our latest releases and our monthly bargain books visit our website: **saperebooks.com**